The Chosen

The Council of Calamity Trilogy Book 1

PATRICK IOVINELLI

World Castle Publishing, LLC
Pensacola, Florida
Copyright © Patrick Iovinelli
Paperback ISBN: 9781949812053
eBook ISBN: 9781949812060
First Edition World Castle Publishing, LLC, October 22, 2018
http://www.worldcastlepublishing.com
Licensing Notes
Cover: Karen Fuller
Editor: Maxine Bringenberg

Table of Contents

PROLOGUE
GENERATIONS EARLIER

The old man sat upon his bed, listening to the noises of the gathering dark about him. His face was worn with care and he wore a kindly expression, as if he were listening to an old friend describing his ills. Of course, no one could see him because there was no light in his room — the old man was blind.

He often explained to his daughter that at dusk he could hear the clamor of the day subsiding, as if the world was finally exhaling its breath, and then could hear the subtle noises of the night slowly fading into existence.

The wind brushed gently against the thatched roof of their cabin, rustling the straw. The sound wasn't ominous; it was soothing.

His daughter was at the hearth, scooping broth into the clay bowl that her father always used.

"Dear?" She heard the word slither through the darkness and finally stop at the flickering light of the fire. The girl's hands shook as she poured the broth into the bowl.

She swallowed hard, barely able to contain herself. "Coming, Father," she said. Her voice was a loud and striking disturbance into the quiet of the house.

She put her other hand on the bowl to steady herself as she turned toward the darkness and began to take unsteady steps toward her father's room.

"Careful," he called to her.

The girl walked slowly into the room and felt into the darkness until her hand found the table beside her father's bed. She put the bowl gently onto it and felt for the candle. Once she found it, the daughter pressed her thumb and forefinger together and sighed. As she separated her fingers, a tiny flame was suspended between them. She placed it onto the wick of the candle and the flickering glow illuminated the room.

"You didn't use the matches," the old man said. It wasn't a question.

"No."

"You can make the fire at will. Your power is growing. I am proud of you," he said.

"Thank you, Father."

The girl turned toward her father. The flickering candle threw her silhouette against the wall. One side of her thin, pale face lit up and shone against the darkness. A girl of fourteen, she was nearly as tall as her father when he stood, and high cheekbones dominated her pale features, giving the peasant girl the face of a noblewoman. Her clothing betrayed her, though. Her dress, of coarse fabric and broad hand stitching, was worn and faded. It had been made by her mother many years before.

She stared down at the figure of the old man, sitting stiffly on the end of his bed. The daughter realized that many years before he must have been handsome and strong, but now, his body was withered, and his hair was a dirty gray. The girl realized that he was only forty-seven or forty-eight, but he looked like he was older than sixty. The power had drained his strength and stolen years from him.

"Father, what did that man want today?" The girl thought about the man who had come to see her father earlier in the day. He was a young man, in his twenties, but his body was thin and weary. He moved slowly, and his hands were covered in dark spots. They rarely had visitors, but this anxious man had come in frantically, nearly hysterical. It had been several minutes before they calmed him down, and then the old man had sent his daughter outside, so that the young man and the old could speak in the privacy of the kitchen. Of course, she sat beneath the window and listened.

"What they all want," he said. The old man shook his head sadly. "He has the power and uses it to his advantage, but he has just begun to understand that the power comes with a price. Every time a person uses his power, it drains some of his essence, his strength, his life. Such is the nature of magic. If we are judicious, and use it sparingly, it can aid us in the most difficult times of our lives, and we will maintain our strength and the years may remain stretched before us. However, if we use it too often or for purposes too strictly aligned against the laws of nature and life, it will strike us down like a plague sent from the gods."

"Is there no way to use the power without consequence?"

The old man smiled. "Ahh. You too, dear?"

"I was just wondering if it could be done," she said quickly.

"There are legends of some of our kind who have found ways to use the power and have maintained their strength and life, but they always end badly, driven insane by their power or their need to hold on to it. No. It is better to take what the power offers us thankfully, and leave the rest alone." As he said this, the old man ran his fingers gently over his clouded, vacant eyes.

7

"Is that how you lost your sight, Father?" she asked.

"I have promised for many years to tell you how I lost my sight. At last, my dear, I believe that you are old enough to understand." The old man bent his head forward and took a deep breath.

"You were still small, maybe two or three years old, when your mother took sick. She began to sweat in the night and have pains in her stomach. At first they were mild, and she told me not to worry about them. Her fits frightened you, though, so we sent you to your aunt's to stay until the illness passed. After a few days, they got worse and I brought her into the village to see the doctor. A grave little man, he said that your mother had contracted some infection that he had no power to cure. He offered her a tonic that might ease her stomach pains, but there was nothing he could do to stop such sickness.

"As we sat in his home and the doctor examined your mother and took her blood into vials, the doctor's wife stood in the doorway of the room, watching. I took little notice of her, so concerned was I for your mother. The doctor needed to mix the tonic for your mother and boil it in the hearth, but he could not find matches. Without a thought, I made flames appear in the fireplace. The doctor stopped and stared at me in amazement, but said nothing. After a moment, he continued his mixture. I looked up briefly at his wife. The woman's jaunty face had been passive throughout the entire examination, but then it creased into a look of wonder and she gripped the wall with trembling fingers. I thought she was merely afraid after seeing my magic. I quickly looked away from her and did not bring my eyes to her face again. A few minutes later, she had disappeared from the doorway.

"The doctor administered the tonic and it calmed your mother's pain. He gave us the rest in a bottle and apologized for not being able to help us more. I said nothing, but your mother embraced the doctor and told him that we were forever grateful for his help, and that the greatest kindness a person could do was to ease another's suffering.

"We went home and I dutifully administered the tonic to your mother, but after a few days, the sickness grew stronger and the tonic failed to ease her pain. I sent a boy to the doctor telling him about your mother's condition and asking him for a stronger tonic. A half hour later, there was a knock at the door. Your mother's pain was so great that she had passed out from it, but she was still moving fitfully in her uneasy slumber. I ran to the door expecting the doctor, but I was surprised to find his wife, wrapped in a heavy gray shawl against the autumn chill, on the doorstep.

"I invited her in and asked if she had sent word from her husband. She told me that her husband was away seeing another patient in the village, but that she might offer some assistance.

"'Do you assist your husband in his practice?' I asked.

"'No,' she said.

"'Then how can you help?' I asked, rather rudely.

"She stared into my face for a long while, seeming to search for something in my eyes. Finally, she said, 'You have the power.'

"'Yes,' I said, and stood up.

"'You can use it to save her,' she said.

"'How do you know?' I asked.

"She stood and unwrapped her shawl. From within it floated a book. A heavy tome with a black leather cover moved through the air before me. I stood amazed. I looked from the book to the doctor's wife.

"Finally, the book floated down onto the table and opened.

9

The pages rippled, then stopped. I took one last look at the woman and sat back down. I looked at the page and it was a spell, but more complex than I had ever seen. I read it over and over again. It was a siphoning spell. If I performed the spell correctly, it would siphon the illness from your mother's body. However powerful the spell, its warning was even more so. The last line written after the spell read simply, 'Whosoever shall take the essence of another must give of himself.'

"I understood. If I were to use the spell to save your mother, I would suffer greatly. The spell might even kill me, but I didn't care. It was a risk I was willing to take in order to save her.

"I prepared everything. All day I gathered up the necessary items and read the spell until I had it from memory. Meanwhile, your mother's pain grew, and I feared that she might die before I was ready to perform it. That night, I hastened to her bedside and looked upon the woman I loved. She was already gaunt, and her face was spotted and strained from the pain. I put my hand to her forehead. She was burning up. I laid the book next to her and began the incantation.

"As I spoke, her body relaxed and she opened her eyes. They were clouded, but she stared at me. About halfway through the spell, I felt a burning pain in my head — it was beginning. I read on. Suddenly your mother raised her head. The clouds had cleared from her vision, but were replaced by a look of horror. 'No!' she whispered. 'You'll die!' Her voice was still weak, but the clarity of her speech told me that the spell was working. It was then that my eyesight failed. My eyes burned and I closed them, but I knew the spell by heart. I continued the incantation. Then, the burning jolted through my body until I felt it in my chest and my legs. I fell to my knees and felt all life leaving me. Suddenly I felt the soft caress of your mother's hand on my face. Although I was in agony, I was happy. I thought she would live. Then the burning rushed back through my body until it reached the point upon which your mother's hand was on me. I felt a flash of the most horrible pain I've ever felt, and then suddenly, nothing. The pain left me. I could feel your mother's hand tense up, and she writhed wildly as the pain that had been coursing through me struck her frail body. She screamed. It was a piercing, painful shriek, and it tore my heart to pieces. Then I heard her body fall back on the bed. I knew she was dead."

The old man leaned forward and put his hands on his knees. His shoulders slumped and he began to sob. It was as if he'd relived the entire experience in the telling.

His daughter stood silently watching her father. She did not reach out to him. She waited patiently for him to gain control of himself. Once he looked up, she said, "Do you still have the book?"

His sniffling stopped and the old man sat up. "What? Haven't you been listening? I just told you how that terrible spell broke my body, and still didn't save your mother's life."

"Yes. I just wanted to know if you still had the book with that spell in it," she said. Her eyes gleamed like emeralds in the flickering light of the candle in her father's room.

"Of course not," the old man said. He coughed uneasily.

"You look very tired, Father," his daughter said. "You should take your broth and then rest."

The old man paused for a moment. He held his head high as if to peer into her face, but that was impossible. He slumped low again. "Yes. Yes. You're right. Thank you, dear. You are a good and dutiful daughter."

"Thank you, Father," she said, and left him alone in the room.

The girl walked swiftly down to her own room off the

11

kitchen, then turned and listened. She could hear her father fall to his knees and slide out the box from beneath his bed. She heard him shuffle furiously through the contents and then suddenly stop. He had found what he was looking for. The girl imagined him softly running his hands over the worn leather on the cover of the spell book. That would satisfy him. He would put it away, confident that she was never going to find it.

The girl went to her own bed and picked up the pillow. She reached into the case and pulled out a book without a cover. It was an ancient book with thick, yellow pages, handwritten in a formal, flowing script. The girl flipped through the pages. She found the siphoning spell quickly. She'd read it dozens of times already.

The daughter smirked as she thought, *So this was the spell that Father used to try and save Mother.* She had been thinking about using this exact spell, but for a different purpose. The girl sat up for a while, reading the spell over and over again. Soon she would do it. Now that she understood how it worked, she was certain that there was no danger whatsoever. She only needed one more thing. When the girl finally went to bed, all her worries and fears were gone. She slept a peaceful, dreamless sleep.

The next morning, she rose early. The old man was still dozing as his daughter dressed and left the house. She looked down at the village of Coyne from just outside their cottage. The buildings were old and weathered, scattered around the square. Already the townsfolk were rising and heading toward their fields or shops, ready to work until sunset.

The girl saw a cart tip as it was being pulled by an ox, its contents spilling all over the muddy road. She watched small, hooded peasants struggle to right the cart and collect the grain and straw. She spat on the ground before her. Soon, she would

12

be away from this place. Forever.

The girl walked in the opposite direction from the village to the woods. She didn't follow the path — she didn't need to. The girl had spent many hours wandering the woods, and knew every tree and flower within them. She walked north until she came to the bushes near the clearing, and approached them slowly. The girl took out the book and found the page she was looking for. In the corner was a sketch of a purple flower, its pistil a black cylinder, hardly distinguishable in the flowing petals. She bent down to examine the flowers within the bush. There could be no mistake. They were the same. The flowers were monkshood. The girl picked several of them and placed them in a small pouch at her belt.

When she returned home, her father was sitting at the small table in the kitchen. He was pulling apart a loaf of bread and chewing the pieces noisily.

"Is that you, dear?" he asked between mouthfuls.

"Yes, Father."

His brows furrowed in concentration. "You were up early. Why? Are you all right?"

"Yes, Father. I just couldn't sleep." The girl didn't look at the old man. She rushed past him into her room and shut the door. The old man went on chewing.

The girl put her small pouch on the bed and went to the writing table under the window. Her father had built it for her mother many years ago. It was worn, but the workmanship was beautiful. There were flowers carved into the joint covers, and the legs looked like tree trunks covered in vines. It even had a rolling cover that locked. She took the small key from her pocket and unlocked the cover to the writing table. As she rolled the cover back, she looked at the various items and ingredients she would need for both the monkshood potion and the siphoning

13

spell.

At dusk, the girl found her father sitting on the grass outside their small cottage. His face was raised toward the setting sun. He appeared to be warming himself in its glow.

"Father, your broth," the daughter said.

"Thank you, dear. Help me up, please."

The girl came forward and reached for the old man's outstretched hands, and as she pulled him up he stumbled forward into her arms.

"Sorry," he muttered.

"It's fine, Father," she said.

"I don't know what I'd do without you," he said.

But the girl had already gone back into the house.

Inside, the old man seated himself at the table before his broth. The girl sat opposite him. There was nothing on the table in front of her.

He took a spoonful into his mouth. "It's tart," he said. He listened for a moment. "Why aren't you eating, dear?"

"I'm not hungry," she said. Her hands gripped the table so hard that her fingernails pressed into the wood. "You should eat, Father. You need your strength."

"I suppose," he said, and took another spoonful. Three more times he brought the spoon to his lips. Silence. He looked up toward his daughter. "I...I don't feel well," he said thickly.

The girl said nothing.

The old man stood up quickly, knocking over his chair. He was breathing heavily, and his hands began to shake. "What's happening?" He lunged across the table and reached for his daughter. "What's happening?"

The girl leapt backward out of her chair and her father's reach. She looked upon his bent figure, huddled over the table, feebly reaching for her as the monkshood potion coursed through his body and slowly drained the feeling from his limbs. He banged his hand furiously against the table, trying to restore the feeling. He picked his head up toward her. "Vi—?" he began. Then he collapsed onto the table.

The girl dragged his frail body from the kitchen into her bedroom and laid him roughly in the bed. He could not move nor speak, but his unseeing eyes darted rapidly about trying to make sense of what was happening. She saw his body tense up as he tried to scream.

"I suppose you're wondering what I've done to you, Father," she said.

Her father's pupils were tiny pits of fear beneath the milky film that rendered him sightless. She moved about the room quickly and surely. She had planned this for months, and had gone through the process in every minute detail so many times that it was second nature. Still, the girl could hardly contain her excitement as she laid the bone, the feathers, and the small bowl filled with her own blood on to the bed next to her father's rigid body.

"I've given you a small dose of the monkshood potion," she said.

After a few seconds of silence, her father released his breath heavily.

"You've seen it before, haven't you?" she said as she moved about the room, making preparations.

She pulled open his shirt and dipped her fingers in the bowl of her own blood. She smeared her blood onto his forehead, his wrists, and over his heart. His body tensed again, trying to speak, but the potion was strong. The paralysis still held him within its grip.

"I found it in your book months ago, Father," she said. "I figured it would be the perfect way to incapacitate you without killing you. You have to be alive for me to perform the siphoning spell on you."

A small grunt escaped his lips. Suddenly, his daughter looked down at him. He was already coming out of it. The potion wouldn't hold the old man much longer. His lips moved again, and a single word escaped them: "Why?"

"When I found your book," she said, "I knew you wouldn't want me to have it, so I removed the cover and sewed it onto the spine of another book. I believe you have *The Adventures of Pirate Jack* hidden under your bed as we speak. When I found it, I knew there was more to magic than making sparks or lifting spoons off the table. You were trying to keep me from realizing my power!" The girl couldn't hide the selfish anger within her voice as she ground the bone, feathers, and herbs into the bowl with her blood.

"No...protect...," was all he could manage to say. His hand rose feebly off the bed. He held it out toward his daughter. The fingers twitched.

"Protect?" the girl laughed. It was a high, creaking sound that came wheezily from the back of her throat. She bent close to his face. "I figured it out, Father. I know how to use my power without consequence. I will use the siphoning spell like you used it on poor Mother." She held up the book, ready to read the incantation. "Except instead of siphoning the sickness out of you, I'm going to take your power for myself."

"No...kill you...." He raised his hand higher, and was able to turn his head toward his daughter.

"Oh no, Father. I understand now," she said. "Your little story yesterday told me everything I need to know."

With that, the girl took a step back and began to read the incantation. A single tear fell down the old man's face as he lay there, listening to his daughter. He strained and tried to reach

16

her, but he couldn't. His muscles still wouldn't respond to his commands.

The girl read on, and as she reached the middle of the incantation, she felt the burning pain her father had described. It was as if someone was touching her head with a firebrand. She felt her knees buckling, but she wouldn't give in. The girl remained standing. She was strong where her father had been weak. The girl read on, and as the pain began to course through her body she reached out and touched her father's outstretched hand. Suddenly the pain shot toward her hand, and she felt the pulsating burn pass into his fingertips and through his body. The daughter held his hand tightly as he writhed in agony. As she finished the spell, he began to convulse as the pain tore his body, his mind, his spirit to pieces.

Finally, he lay still in the bed. The girl let go of his limp hand and took a step back. She dropped the book to the floor and raised her hand, and the entire bed rose from the ground and hung just below the ceiling of her bedroom in their little cottage.

The girl laughed again, relishing the power she had just taken from her father. She twisted her wrist and the bed spun in the air like a piece of cloth blown by a dry wind. She closed her fist and the bed came crashing down.

The body of her father rolled out of the bed and hit the floor. His milky eyes stared vacantly at the ceiling — into nothingness.

CHAPTER 1
FLYNN HOUSE

Alexa Flynn stood on the porch of her house, sweeping dust and rocks from the steps, chilled by the early morning wind. She lifted her eyes over the fields toward the sliver of sunlight that had just appeared. Alexa leaned the broom against the railing and smoothed the front of her dress. She knew that he would pass by any moment. He always passed their house just when the sun came up.

She picked up the broom again and stepped down into the yard to sweep the walkway. The grass was overgrown and dandelions poked their sunny heads through the tangled green. Alexa's father always complained about the weeds, but she'd always rather liked the dandelions. In fact, one of the first really detailed drawings Alexa had ever done was of a dandelion she'd picked. She remembered how she struggled to create the scraggly green fringe that surrounded the yellow center, and how she'd spent hours trying to give a third dimension to the leaves on its stem. When she'd finished everyone in the family had been impressed, and it was the first time her father had ever mentioned sending her to school.

She turned toward the house and examined it as the sun lit up its façade. The planks of weathered wood splintered and bowed in some places, particularly under the left side of the porch. The front door stood out against the wood. It was a dark green, freshly painted by her father just a few days before.

It was a small cabin with a pitched roof, but there was a second floor, with comfortable bedrooms and the brick hearth her father had built himself right in the center. It wasn't much, but it was home.

As she was looking at the chipped bricks at the top of the chimney, Alexa heard a voice from behind her. "It's a nice place to live, isn't it?"

Alexa turned to face a tall boy in an oversized shirt tucked into worn brown pants rolled up below his knees. He wore no shoes, but carried them in his left hand. His long face was freckled from hours in the sun. Alexa knew that Duster was older than she was, but she could never be quite sure how much. He could've been anywhere from sixteen to twenty-two or twenty-three. Alexa had once asked her father how old Duster was, and he'd said that he was sure that Duster was only a year or two older than Alexa, whose sixteenth birthday was within the next month. Duster had eyes of icy blue that looked older and wearier than a boy's.

Alexa drew herself up to her full height. "Yes. Yes it is," she said with striking formality. She was trying to act mature, but when Duster smirked at her, she knew he saw through it and Alexa felt ridiculous.

Duster nodded at her and took a step as if he were going to continue on his way out to the fields.

"How are you this morning?" Alexa blurted out quickly.

"Fine, thanks. And you, Alexa?" he said, still smirking.

Duster had been leaning on one leg in a comfortable pose

19

when he suddenly stood erect. He wasn't looking at Alexa any more.

"Good morning, Mr. Flynn," he said.

Alexa heard her father's gruff baritone behind her. "Hello, Duster. On your way out to the fields, and you stopped here to chat up my daughter?"

Alexa dropped her head and sighed.

"No, sir. It's nothing like that. I was just making friendly conversation. I—"

John Flynn laughed suddenly. "Relax, boy. I love making you sweat is all."

Duster's face relaxed a little. He looked back down at Alexa. "Well, have a good day, Alexa." He looked past her again. "You too, sir." He gave a quick wave and continued on down the road past the Flynn house toward the fields.

Alexa turned around and saw her burly father, his arms folded, staring after the boy as he continued down the path. There was a look of consternation on his face until Duster had gotten a little farther away, then his weathered face split into a grin. He rubbed his short brown beard as he watched Duster's retreating figure.

Alexa put her hands on her hips. "Must you always do that?" she said.

"I can't help it," her father said, finally looking at his daughter. His dark, piercing eyes lit on her with amused affection. He took lumbering steps down the stairs. "Oh, what's the matter? Did your old dad interrupt your little romantic moment?"

Alexa turned back to him sweeping with vigor. "Oh please," she said. "It was nothing like that."

When John Flynn reached her, he put his arm around Alexa's shoulder. They both looked up to the point where

Duster had disappeared around the hill. "Oh, don't worry. He's a good boy," he said. "Nice to look at, too, huh?"

His daughter shook him off and took up her sweeping again.

"He's a sad story, though," John said to himself.

Alexa stopped and looked up at him. "Why?" Her father didn't answer right away. He seemed to be thinking something over to himself. "Father?" Alexa urged him.

John shook his head and looked at Alexa. "You remember that Duster and his mother came to the farm just a couple of years ago. They were nearly starved when they came here, and they begged Mr. Eckerly to let them settle on his land and mind it in exchange for their service. Eckerly, of course, didn't want to. A widow and her teenage son are hardly valuable workers, but Duster begged. I remember Duster telling old Eckerly that he could do the work of four men. Eckerly laughed, but said that he couldn't pass up such a bargain and gave him a chance. His mother wasn't nothing to scream about, but that boy...that boy could work. It's like he never got tired. The sun would be setting and everyone else would be dragging themselves home, and Duster would stay behind and organize things for Mr. Eckerly. He was smart, too. He figured out ways to get water to some of the outer fields from the river by digging ditches."

John Flynn paused and shook his head. "Duster worked and worked, and nobody even noticed for a while. But a few months ago his mother stopped coming into the fields to work. I asked him about it and he said not to tell anyone, but she was sick. Real sick.

"Now I didn't say anything to anyone except your mother, but every once in a while, if I saw him alone, I would ask Duster how she was. He usually just shook his head. Then one day I saw Mr. Eckerly out riding early in the morning. He stopped and told me to wash up and come out to Duster's house when I was done feeding the pigs. I did, and I found Mr. Eckerly and Duster standing in front of a grave. Duster must have dug it himself and buried his mother all alone."

"That's terrible, Dad. How long ago was that?" Alexa asked.

"About a month."

"And we didn't go to the funeral? Mother didn't bake bread for him?" Alexa wiped at the corner of her eye.

"He didn't want anything," her father said. "Even old Eckerly, whose generosity doesn't usually extend beyond his eyebrows, offered him a couple of days off. Duster said he didn't want them. He told Mr. Eckerly that he just wanted to work, like always. Your mother was so upset. She made me bring her over there the next morning, and we brought bread and even a small cake. Duster was real nice about it, but he half rushed us out of the house because he didn't want to be late for work. He thanked us about a dozen times. Your mother asked him to come to dinner, or if he would like to take the room in our attic, as to not be so lonesome. He got a little choked up, but said that he couldn't."

Alexa thought about Duster. She'd been so focused on his easy movements, and how his lip quirked up handsomely when he smiled, that she felt guilty for not trying to see Duster's situation and to understand his life.

Her father interrupted her thoughts suddenly. "Then he started walking by here on his way to and from work," he said.

"What?" Alexa said.

"Well, Duster can get to the fields and the barn much more quickly by following the river. That's the way he always walked, until just after his mother died. I noticed that he's started taking the long way back and forth." John Flynn raised an eyebrow. "You know, right past our house." He turned and went back

22

into the house.

A few hours later, Miriam Flynn had just placed the large iron pan with the day's bread in the hearth. She flexed one of her bony shoulders. The house was stiflingly warm. The plain wooden planks seemed to heave inwardly, as if trying to catch their breath against the summer heat and the warm hearth. She turned the soft oval of her face toward her daughter as Alexa wiped the sweat off her forehead while she sat at the table with a book.

"Go sit outside, sweetheart," her mother said, wiping her slender hands on a towel.

"It's just as hot out there," Alexa began. "And besides, Michael's outside."

Miriam Flynn went to the window and looked out. "I don't see him." Her brows were furrowed in concentration.

Alexa looked out the window, too. "He's out there," she said. "Dad sent him home again because he was napping under a tree instead of working out in the fields."

Miriam went to the door and opened it. "Michael! Michael!"

Alexa's twin came around from the other side of the house. Michael had a long pointed nose and dark eyes under wavy brown hair. He strolled over with his hands in his pockets, then came and stood before his mother. Michael was nearly a foot taller than she was.

Miriam looked up at her son. "Michael, what are you doing here? Shouldn't you be working?"

"Dad sent me home. I went off to the trees to get out of the sun for a few minutes, and the next thing I know, I'm asleep on the ground. Then suddenly, Dad's shaking me and cursing up a storm. I tried to explain that it was an accident, but he just wouldn't listen. He called me a disgrace and raised his hand like he was going to hit me until I ran. I'm not going back out there today."

"No. That's probably for the best," Miriam said. "If you go back out there today he'll probably just get on you again."

"I know I made a mistake, but he never gives me a chance —" Michael began.

Miriam cut him off. "You've made plenty of mistakes before, Michael Flynn." Her eyes softened. "Did you eat? I'll bet he chased you off the fields before lunch."

Michael lowered his gaze and shook his head.

"Come along, dear," Miriam said. "Don't worry about your father. He's hard on you because he wants you to do well. He wants you to become a good, dependable worker so that one day you can support your own family."

"My own family? Why would I want my own family? I'm not going to marry some farm girl and have babies so that I can work on some wealthy landowner's property until I die. I'm getting out of here as soon as I can," Michael said.

Miriam shook her head and went into the house.

Michael stood there for a moment and then turned to look out over the fields. Alexa appeared in the doorway behind him. "You shouldn't say those things to Mom," Alexa said.

Michael didn't turn to face his sister. "Why not? It's true. I'm not staying here."

"They need you to work, Michael," Alexa said.

"You can work in the fields," he said.

"You know they won't let me," Alexa said.

"Oh, that's right. Saint Alexa can't work out in the fields. She's got to focus on her studies because Mom and Dad, who can barely afford soap and grain, are going to somehow come up with enough money to send her off to Bentham Academy." Michael turned on her. His face contorted into a mocking sneer and his voice rose to a squawking imitation of his mother. "But

Alexa can read and write, and sing, and draw. She's going to be a teacher or a clerk, or queen of the Southern Provinces."

"Shut up!" Even though Michael towered over her, Alexa pushed him with both hands. He stumbled backward a few steps.

Miriam rushed out the door and came between them. She put both of her hands on Michael's chest to hold him back. Her lined face strained up at her son's. "You two need to stop this!"

"She always comes to the aid of her favorite!" Michael sneered over his mother's head at Alexa.

Suddenly, Miriam's hand came up and slapped Michael across the face. Michael took a step back. Both he and Miriam looked shocked. She had never hit either of the children before.

"Michael, I'm sorry!" she said.

Michael turned and ran off down the path toward the fields.

"Michael!" Miriam called after him.

"I'll get him," Alexa said, and ran past her mother.

Michael was taller and took great strides, so Alexa lost sight of him pretty quickly, but she had a good idea where he had gone. Once she realized that she wasn't going to catch him, she slowed to a walk and began the trek toward the grove.

Just beyond the fields to the west there was a great woodland, with mighty oaks and beeches that stretched for miles. About half a mile into it, there was a grove of smaller oaks with branches that started much lower to the ground. Michael and Alexa had discovered it years ago, and since they could pull themselves into the trees and climb, it became a favorite place of theirs to play.

Even now, when either of them needed to get away from the house, they usually still returned to the grove. Alexa hadn't been there since the previous summer, but she had a feeling Michael still frequented their old haunt.

When Alexa finally came to the edge of the woodland, she was glad to have some relief from the burning sun. There was a mild breeze among the leaves, and it was much cooler. She walked along the familiar path and recognized all of the landmarks. The hill that had two large rocks resting on its top, which Michael had named Camel's Hill, was exactly as Alexa remembered it.

It became very dark as she went deeper. Alexa snaked around the fallen trees and headed toward where she thought the grove would be. But something was wrong.

As she came upon it, light blazed into an area that had been cleared of trees. She approached it slowly until she came to its edge. There was no mistake about it: this was the grove, but the trees were gone.

It was strange because none of the areas around it were cleared, just the grove. Alexa took a step into it and saw Michael at its far end, whirling around and looking at the grove in shock, just like her.

"Michael! What happened to the grove?"

He walked toward her. "I don't know."

"But who did this?" Alexa asked.

"I have no idea. I was here last week and the trees were here. I climbed into one of our trees and hid from Dad all afternoon. Who could clear these trees and drag them out of here without us knowing about it?"

Alexa looked around. All that was left were some stumps, but Alexa noticed that they were arranged strangely. Each of four stumps sat about ten feet from its neighbor in a half circle, while a fifth sat directly in front of the semicircle. Alexa tried to remember, but she couldn't picture whether or not the trees were arranged that way when they had been there.

Alexa finally tore her eyes from the stumps and turned to

her brother. "Michael, Mom didn't mean to hit you."

Michael smirked. "Sure."

"Michael, she was just—" Alexa began.

Michael interrupted her. "Do you think they'll do it for me?"

"Do what?" Alexa asked.

"Do you think they're planning to send me to Bentham so that I can become a teacher or an actor and I can get out of this miserable place?"

Alexa lowered her eyes.

"You know they won't," Michael said. He stalked around, kicking stones.

Alexa cleared her throat. "You know, you've never given Mom and Dad a chance to see your talents."

"What talents? It's just unfair…I mean, I can read and write like you, but I'm not good at anything, really." This was one of the few times her tall, lanky brother looked his age. He hunched his shoulders and seemed to shrink into himself.

"I'll bet you've got lots of talents, Michael. You just never try," Alexa said quickly.

"Maybe not," Michael said darkly. "I can't sing or play the violin like you. I can't tell stories, and I don't know the names of every flower in the universe."

Alexa put her hands on her hips. "I didn't learn any of that stuff right away. You have to read about them. You have to practice."

"I don't want to."

"Well, now you're just being a…," Alexa began.

Michael rushed toward her and grabbed her arm. "A what, Alexa? A what?"

As soon as Michael touched her, Alexa felt a searing pain tear into her arm. "Michael, stop! You're hurting me!"

Michael held on even tighter and brought his face right down to hers. "Go on! Tell me what I am!"

Alexa felt the spit hit the side of her face, but she didn't care. She reached over with her left hand and struggled to loosen Michael's grip, but he was too strong. After a few seconds, the pain was too much for Alexa and she fell to her knees.

Michael suddenly let go. When Alexa looked up at him, the anger was gone from his face. His mouth was open and he was staring at her arm. The sleeve of her dress was scorched through, and there was a blistered red burn on her arm in the shape of Michael's hand.

They both stared at it. Alexa's shock temporarily made her forget about her pain. "What did you do?"

"I don't...I don't know." Michael's face was white as he stared at the burn. "I'm sorry," he said.

Michael reached down to help his sister up, but Alexa scrambled to her feet and took several staggering steps back. "Don't!" Alexa's face was strained with panic. She quickly looked around. Michael could tell that she was deciding whether or not to run away from him.

"All right," Michael said, "I won't touch you. Alexa, I'm sorry. I don't know what happened."

Alexa stared at Michael's hand. She didn't say anything.

Michael quickly put the hand behind his back. "Alexa!" he said, trying to snap her out of it. She looked up into his face again. "We should probably go home and treat that burn," he said.

All Alexa could do was nod.

Michael turned in the direction of their house and waved her forward. "Come on," he said gently.

Alexa looked straight ahead as she walked next to Michael through the forest. They didn't speak until they reached the edge and were about to enter the fields. Michael stopped and looked down at his hand.

"What are we going to tell Mom?" he said.

"We'll tell them we built a fire and that I got too close and a spark caught my sleeve," Alexa said.

"But what...." Michael swallowed, "What if it happens again?"

Alexa finally turned to look at him. "Show me your hand."

Michael put his palm up toward her. She leaned over and looked closely at it. She put her hand near it. "It doesn't feel warm."

Alexa's hand hovered for a moment near his, and then she placed her palm to his. Even though Alexa had been fairly sure that whatever it was that had caused Michael to burn her was not present any more, she felt her body relax. "It's okay. Your hand is fine now." She reached down and grabbed the other one. "They're both fine."

"What happened?" Michael said.

"I don't know, Michael. But whatever it was, it's over," she said, and walked forward toward home.

Michael watched Alexa walk slowly forward out into the open, and then looked down into his hands.

"Michael!" He looked up. Alexa had stopped and turned back to him. "You ruined my favorite dress, you know."

She smiled at him, and he couldn't help smiling back. He jogged forward to catch up to her as they headed home.

Chapter 2
Gathering Dark

The Flynns were less talkative than usual as they sat around their scrubbed wooden table for dinner. The day had been hot, and John was tired and sore. He didn't eat much, but refilled his wooden cup with water several times. Miriam kept glancing up at him, waiting for him to tell them about his day in the fields, and to give the family the general news of Mr. Eckerly's farm.

Miriam had noticed that Alexa and Michael had been unusually quiet after they returned from the woods. Michael had simply nodded when she apologized for slapping him, and patted her awkwardly on the back as she leaned in to hug him. It was as she broke from Michael that she noticed the hole in Alexa's dress and the red burn beneath it. They had given her some story about Alexa getting too close to the fire they'd built in the woods, but she knew they were lying. Why would they build a fire on such a hot day? She didn't press them. It was obvious that neither one wanted to tell what happened out beyond the fields.

Miriam had washed the burn gently and treated it with an herbal ointment that seemed to help cuts and scratches heal.

She didn't know what to do for burns. Alexa had grimaced, but said that it didn't hurt that badly. She also made Alexa change out of her dress so that she could patch it. Alexa sat in an old blouse of her mother's and a pair of her own field pants that were from two summers before, so they were very short on her. Alexa was sure that if Michael hadn't been so preoccupied, he'd have made fun of her for wearing such ridiculous clothes.

John didn't seem to notice any of this as he sat wearily in his chair. The sun had set nearly a half an hour earlier.

**

Alexa asked to be excused and went outside to watch the pink dusk dissolve into an inky sea of stars.

It had cooled down outside the house. The wind blew briskly and rustled the grass blades on either side of the path. Alexa sat down and kicked off her shoes. She loved the prickly feel of the grass on her feet.

Suddenly a small dark figure emerged on the path from the fields, and without even being able to make out his shape, Alexa knew it was Duster. Alexa would be able to tell his easy, loping strides anywhere.

As he approached, Alexa had the feeling that Duster thought he was alone. He seemed to be looking at the house behind her. Alexa thought that maybe the failing light and the fact that she was motionless on the grass made it hard for him to see her.

Suddenly Duster stopped on the path and stared at her house. He turned his head a little, as if he was straining to hear something from within. Alexa cocked her head slightly as well, but could hear nothing. After a moment Duster shook his head and began to walk on.

He was nearly even with her when suddenly, Alexa decided to speak. "Evening, Duster."

31

He jumped. "Alexa, is that you?"

"Yes. Sorry. I didn't mean to frighten you," she said. Alexa wondered if he could see her grinning in the shadows.

"Oh, I wasn't frightened or anything," he said quickly. "I just didn't know anyone was out here."

"Sure," Alexa said. Alexa watched the dark shape shuffle, but Duster said nothing. "Why did you stop to listen to our house?" she asked.

"I don't know. I like to hear the sounds of the family dinner. People talking and laughing. Your house is especially quiet tonight," he said.

"Yeah. Dad was tired from the heat, and Michael and I had been arguing earlier today." Then Alexa stopped. "What do you mean we're 'especially quiet tonight?' Do you listen to our house every night when you pass by?"

"Well. Sort of, I guess. I don't mean to do it. I don't mean any harm by it. It's just—" Duster stopped. Alexa thought he was searching for the right words.

She urged him on. "It's just what?"

"I don't know. It's just that my house is quiet. Sometimes I just miss the sounds of...." He trailed off.

Alexa thought about Duster's home. It was a small cottage a half a mile from their house, built from greying timbers. Alexa had never been inside, but she imagined this boy, sitting alone eating his dinner by the light of a single candle while the dark gathered around him, staring across the table at his mother's empty chair.

Alexa tried to finish the sentence for him. "Of family?"

"Yeah."

Alexa stood up. "Dad told me about your mother. I'm sorry."

Duster whispered, "Thank you."

They stood in silence for a while. Finally, Alexa said, "You know, Dad told me that you've been invited to dinner. Why don't you come in now? I'm sure there's plenty left."

"No, that's okay. Thank you anyway," he said, and Alexa saw Duster's dark shape start to move off past her house.

"Good night, Duster," she called into the darkness.

Alexa couldn't see him anymore, but she heard him stop. "Good night, Alexa."

As the words reached her from the darkness, Alexa could hear something in them. There was something sad or desperate in the words, but she couldn't quite put her finger on it. As his footsteps faded, she stood for a long while after trying to figure out what it was.

Alexa went back inside and found her father sitting alone at the table. Her mother was at the basin scrubbing bowls. Michael was lying on the rug next to the hearth, which was dark and empty at the moment.

John Flynn seemed to have recovered himself a bit after a few bites and many cups of water. He was grinning at Alexa.

"Duster?" was all he said.

"Yes." Alexa shook her head. Her father stifled a small laugh. Alexa couldn't help smiling back at him a little.

"Michael," he called suddenly.

Michael got up slowly and walked back over to the table. He wouldn't look at his father. "Yes."

"Sit down, boy," he barked.

"John!" Miriam said sharply.

"All right, all right," John sighed. "Please sit down, Michael."

A little surprised, Michael looked up at his father as he sat across from him.

"Michael," John began. He stopped and cocked his head

to the side, searching for the right words. "Your mother told me about you and Alexa this morning. Now, we all know that your sister is a very talented girl, and we've been talking about sending her to Bentham for a while now. But you must understand something, son. You've got to show them superior talents to get into a place like that. You can't...." He trailed off.

"I know. I can't do anything." Michael looked at Alexa as he said it.

Miriam turned and came over to Michael. She put her hand on his shoulder. "It's not like we want this life for you, Michael. We want you to have opportunities, too. You have a whole year before they will make any decisions, but you need to develop your abilities. You need to start learning more subjects and studying them seriously. You need to read more books. I'm sure Alexa will lend you some of hers—"

Michael cut her off. "So if I qualify, you'll send me to Bentham, too?"

Miriam smiled. "Yes," she said.

"How will you pay for it? How will you pay for both of us to go?" Michael said.

John shook his head. "We don't know yet. Eighty silver for the term is almost twice what we make with Mr. Eckerly—and that's for each of you. We've been saving as much as we can for Alexa the last couple of years, but I'm not sure it'll be enough."

Michael stood up. He looked from his father to his mother. "Thank you for the offer, but you don't have to worry about me."

"Michael—" John began.

"It's all right, Dad," Michael said. "Good night."

Michael walked quickly into his room and closed the door. They all listened for a moment, but they heard nothing except the rustle of clothing, and in a matter of moments, the candlelight was extinguished and they could see only darkness from the outline of his door.

The next day John left shortly after sunrise, leaving Alexa and Miriam doing their morning work. Alexa was beating out the rug in front of the house when Michael came out.

"Good morning," she said without looking at him.

Michael didn't say anything. She turned to look at him, framed in the doorway. He had obviously just woken up. His hair was ruffled and he yawned dramatically. He reached up and put his hands on the top of the doorframe and stretched his torso. Alexa had to remind herself that she was annoyed with Michael, or else she would've laughed at his morning manner.

Suddenly they both heard the sounds of a horse coming down the path from the open country to the south of Mr. Eckerly's farm. They turned and watched as a small wagon, filled with straw, creaked along the road, pulled by a large and forbidding mare. As it came closer, they could see two men riding in the cart. They were dressed in the coarse brown robes of monks, but something about their manner told Alexa that these were not religious men. The driver, a swarthy-faced man with ragged eyebrows, waved brightly at Alexa and Michael as they approached.

Alexa folded the rug and held it against her as the man pulled the cart to a stop in front of their house.

"Good morning, children," the driver said. His voice was as coarse as his robes.

"Good morning," Michael and Alexa said together.

"Is your father home?" the driver asked.

"No, sir," Michael said. Alexa looked up at Michael. She shook her head, but Michael wasn't looking at her.

"Oh, that's good." With that the driver jumped down from the cart. His companion, a pudgy, chinless man, had already walked forward and stood just a few feet from Alexa.

She looked at his robes and suddenly saw the glint of metal among the sleeves of his robes. "Michael!" she screamed.

The pudgy man came forward and clapped a dirty hand to her mouth. He then held up the knife he'd been hiding. He spat into her face, "Not another word!"

The driver hadn't moved—he was staring up at Michael. Meanwhile, another man sat up from the back of the cart. He was older than the others, with a grizzled brown beard spotted with gray. It took the old man a few moments to scramble down. He walked past the driver and walked up the stairs toward Michael.

Suddenly, Miriam appeared in the doorway behind him. "Michael, are you and Alexa talking to someone?" Then she saw the gnarled face of the man on the steps. "Michael, get inside."

"You best do what your mother says, boy," the older man said in a creaky hiss.

But Michael didn't move. Now he looked down at Alexa, who had tears streaming down her cheeks as she stood there with the knife in her face.

"Please don't harm us," Miriam said. "Take whatever you like. Come on, Michael." She pulled Michael back into the house by the shoulder. The pudgy man walked behind Alexa and shoved her hard toward the stairs. She stumbled, but scrambled up the steps quickly. When she got through the door, she ran around the old robber and stood next to her mother.

Miriam reached up and hugged her shoulder. "It's going to be all right," she whispered in Alexa's ear.

"Here's what's going to happen," the old robber said. "You children will sit quietly at the table while my friend here holds this knife to your mother's throat. None of you will move, or fight, or scream, or else she dies."

Michael stepped in front of his mother. "No. Hold the knife to my throat. I promise we won't do anything."

The swarthy-faced driver shoved Michael. "You heard the boss! Sit down, boy!"

Michael made as if he would strike the man, but his mother stopped him. She gently ushered him into a chair at the table.

"No. Do what they say," Miriam said evenly. "It'll all be over sooner if we do what they want."

"You see," the old man said. He leaned down to look in Michael's face. "Mommy knows best." He smiled, revealing a set of badly made wooden dentures.

The pudgy man held the knife to Miriam's throat while Alexa and Michael sat at the table, watching the others rummage through their possessions. They didn't find much: a silver teapot that had belonged to Miriam's mother, a fine silver chain that John had given Miriam years ago before they were married, and a small opal ring that John had given Alexa on her thirteenth birthday.

The old man was stomping around in Alexa's room, apparently very agitated at finding so little in the house. "Books? Is this what you spend your wages on? Books?" he yelled. He came out and pointed a short sword toward Miriam. "Where's your money?" he said.

"We don't have any," Miriam said.

"That's a lie," the old robber said, and he came forward and slapped Miriam across the face.

Michael stood up, but before he could move he felt the point of the swarthy-faced man's short sword in his back. "Sit down," he said. Michael turned to look at him, but sat down.

"Where is it?" the old man screamed again. Alexa saw the spittle hit her mother's cheek.

37

The old man struck Miriam again, this time with the hilt of his sword. Miriam fell to her knees.

"Please stop!" Alexa screamed. "I'll get it!"

"No!" Miriam said thickly.

"Mom, it's all right. I'll get it."

Everyone watched as Alexa got up and walked to her room. They heard her rummaging through the bookshelf, and she came out with a large book with a red cover. She brought it to the old robber, who looked down at it, confused. Alexa shook the book and everyone heard the jingle of coins.

"It's hollow," she said. "It's everything we have." Alexa unfastened the clasp on the cover, revealing bronze and silver coins. The old man looked at it and nodded approvingly.

"Alexa," her mother said, and she began to cry. She fell forward onto her hands. "Please don't take that," she said between sobs.

"It's all right," Alexa said.

Suddenly Michael was up, and he grabbed at the sword hand of the swarthy-faced man, who had been distracted by Alexa. Michael brought his fist down on the robber's hand and the sword clanged to the floor. Then, Michael grabbed at the man's neck and the robber began to scream. Alexa saw the faint glow of Michael's hands as they tore at the man's neck, and as he got a hold of the robber, she saw his flesh burn. The robber screamed and fell to his knees.

The old robber saw the struggle, but quickly snatched the book and pushed Alexa to the floor, yelling to his pudgy companion, "Kill her!"

Before Alexa could move, the pudgy little man raised the knife and brought it down between her mother's shoulder blades. Miriam's head jerked upward. Alexa could see the shock and strain as their eyes met, and then her mother collapsed to the floor.

Michael was still grappling with the swarthy-faced robber, who was flailing wildly, trying to free himself from Michael's burning grip. The robber finally landed a haymaker on the side of Michael's head, and Michael fell to the floor. The robber bolted from the house, and as she crawled toward her mother's body, Alexa heard the cart flying back up the path the way it had come.

When she got to her mother, a dark stain had already spread across the back of her dress. She looked over at Michael, who was staggering to his feet. "Help!"

Michael stumbled over to her and fell on his knees beside Alexa. They rolled Miriam onto to her back and saw that she took struggling, unsteady breaths.

"Mom," Alexa said. Even through her tears, Alexa could see her mother's eyes flittering wildly about the room.

Miriam's hands flailed about as she struggled to move, fighting to keep the life from leaving her slight frame. Then her hands fell to the floor. Miriam breathed in short, sharp gasps, looking up at the faces of her children. She moved her lips, but no sound came out. Blood trickled from the corner of her mouth.

Alexa couldn't look at her any longer. She put her head on her mother's chest. She held it there and listened to the heartbeat, until suddenly, it stopped.

Alexa didn't lift her head for a long time. She held it against her mother's silent breast. The only sound she could hear was Michael sniffling beside her.

CHAPTER 3
THE HALF MOON BRACELET

Alexa and Michael sat alone with their mother's body for a long time. It was nearly noon when they heard footsteps coming up the path from the fields.

Michael got to his feet. "Do you think they've come back? I'll kill 'em!"

Alexa still hadn't raised her head from her mother's bosom. "No. It's Duster," she said. She could hear the easy, measured steps.

Sure enough, Duster's voice emerged from the porch. "Mrs. Flynn? I have a message from Mr. Flynn."

They heard Duster walk up the steps and Alexa didn't look up, but she could tell that his body was blocking out the light streaming in from the doorway. Alexa heard him gasp.

"What happened?" Duster rushed in and knelt down next to Alexa.

"Robbers," Michael said.

Duster said, "Oh no! That's why I'm here. Will Elner's son came running into the field today to tell him that their house had been robbed. They didn't hurt anyone at the Elners', but they took everything of value. It was men dressed like—"

"Monks." Michael finished the sentence for him.

"Yeah." Duster's face was white. He reached out a trembling hand toward Alexa and rested it on her shoulder. "Is she—?" He couldn't finish the question.

Alexa finally picked her head up and looked at Duster. Her eyes were red and swollen, and the single plait she'd had in her hair this morning had been pulled out in the scuffle with the robbers. "She's dead," she said, and collapsed back onto her mother's body. She sobbed uncontrollably.

Michael walked out on to the porch. He sat on the steps and wept.

Duster was still kneeling next to the body with his hand on Alexa's shoulder. He didn't know what to do. He patted her shoulder nervously. "I'm so sorry, Alexa."

Duster stood and pulled Alexa up. She allowed herself to be led to the table. Duster sat her in the chair. She sat staring straight ahead, tears still rolling down her cheeks.

Then Duster went out on to the porch and Alexa heard him talking to Michael. "Come back in and sit with Alexa. I'll go and get your dad. He sent me here to warn you all to stay inside and keep the door locked today after we heard about the Elners. I can't believe this has happened."

Michael staggered in and sat at the table. He stared at his mother's careworn face as she lay on the floor in a pool of her own blood.

Duster ran out of the house and back toward the fields. After only a few minutes, they heard the sound of many horses hurtling down the path and coming to a sudden halt in front of the house. In a moment, their father stood in the doorway looking at the tragic scene before him. He looked at Miriam's body, but then rushed toward the table. He put an arm around both Michael and Alexa. Mr. Eckerly, Duster, and a couple of the other farm hands came in after him.

"Are you children all right?" John asked huskily.

"Fine, Dad," Alexa said. "We're not hurt."

John took Michael's face in his hands and looked him in the eye. "Are you sure?"

Michael nodded. John leaned over and kissed Alexa's forehead. Then he stood erect and turned toward the body of his wife. He walked slowly to her and knelt on the floor. He reached out to touch her face, but he left his hand hovering over it.

He got back to his feet and turned back toward the children. Tears streamed down his face, but there was ferocity in his voice as he spoke. "Who did this?"

"There were three of them," Michael said. "Two were dressed like monks, and the other hid in the back of their cart. They got all of our money. They ran out of here and drove off like maniacs. I think they came from the south."

"I'm going to find them," John said.

Mr. Eckerly came forward and stood next to John. "Yes. We'll set up a search party," he said. "First we have to find out which other houses they robbed, and if there are any other injuries."

John turned on Mr. Eckerly furiously. "The longer we take to get after them, the more likely they are to get away!"

Mr. Eckerly pulled in his chin and rubbed the graying stubble, but said nothing.

Duster stepped forward and whispered urgently to Mr. Eckerly. "Mr. Flynn is right. Let's go. Let's go right now," he said as he moved toward the door.

John Flynn went into the kitchen and pulled the two largest knives from the block on the counter.

"They have swords, Dad," Alexa said as John Flynn went over to the hearth and pulled out the leather wrap with the hewing axe he used to cut down trees and chop firewood.

"That won't matter," John said as he rushed toward the door. Duster followed him, and Michael got to his feet and came forward. John gave one of the kitchen knives to Duster and said, "Get the horses ready." Then, John turned toward his son and put his broad hand on Michael's shoulder. "I'm sorry, son. You can't come," he said gently. Michael opened his mouth to protest, but John stopped him. "Believe me, I understand. You want nothing more than to avenge your mother, but you're too young for this."

"Duster's just a kid, too," Michael said, and tried to push past his father.

"He's two years older than you. He's not a kid any more. He's taken care of his own house for months now. You are forbidden to leave this house until I come back. Do I make myself clear?"

Alexa stood up. "What if you don't?"

John looked quickly at Alexa, and then brought his eyes back to Michael's. "All the more reason for both of you stay here and be safe. Do you two understand?"

Michael put his head down and slumped forward onto John's shoulder. He began to cry. John patted him awkwardly. "I'll be back tonight," he said, and gently pushed Michael away from him.

John turned and rushed out of the house and down to where Duster had the horses waiting. They galloped off toward the south.

The other farm hands who had come walked slowly out of the house, leaving Michael and Alexa alone with Mr. Eckerly. Mr. Eckerly eyed them sadly. "I'm sorry about your mother," he said.

Alexa couldn't say anything, but she nodded.

"I can get the men to carry her out of the house," he said.

Alexa found her voice. "No, sir. Thank you, but that won't be necessary."

Before Mr. Eckerly left, he turned back to Michael and Alexa. "I'll send a boy back here about sundown. I'd like to know that John and Duster have returned."

Alexa nodded.

As soon as Alexa had closed the door behind Mr. Eckerly, Michael rushed off to his room and slammed the door shut. Alexa went slowly to her room and opened the bottom drawer of the clothes chest. She took her extra blanket that she slept with in the winter and brought it to where her mother's body lay. She unfolded it and spread it out on the floor, then pulled her mother's shoulders onto the blanket. Alexa walked around to the other end of her body and dragged her feet on to the blanket before wrapping her neatly in it.

As she prepared to cover her mother's face, she reached down and kissed her cheek. It was still warm. Then she laid the blanket down. She went to the basin and got the bucket and scrub brush, and came back and started to scrub at the pool of blood. It was a slow, arduous task, but Alexa reveled in the work. At least she didn't have to sit there and stare off into the distance, wondering whether or not she would lose both of her parents the same day.

An hour later Alexa found herself outside, wandering the area around her house. She walked a little ways in each direction, but settled on the elm tree about fifty yards to the west of their cabin. She scanned the ground and found a flat spot, untouched by the roots of the great tree, which hung over the earth like an open hand. When her father returned, she would propose that they bury Mother there, comfortably in the shade, but close to her home.

Alexa looked up and found the sun setting beyond the great tree, and she realized that her father had been gone for six or seven hours. Was he still tracking the murderers, or had he and Duster caught up to them?

Alexa tried to find things to do in order to keep herself occupied. She swept the steps again, and began kneading dough for their morning bread. She let the house go entirely dark before she lit one of the small tapers near the washbasin. It flickered feebly and cast shadows on the walls, Alexa's hands, her mother's body—no matter where she looked, the dim flickering shrouded all in shadow and darkness.

It was midnight when John Flynn wearily pushed open the door and came into the house. He looked down at his wife's body, wrapped in Alexa's blanket, and then went to the table. He sat down and laid his axe on the floor. He was grimy and weary, but neither his clothes nor the weapon had any blood on them.

Alexa brought him a plate with bread and cold chicken on it. She poured water into a wooden cup from the carafe, as she had watched her mother do hundreds of times before. It occurred to Alexa that from now on, her mother's household duties were her own.

As she put the plate before her father, she asked, "Did you find them?"

John shook his head, and then in a show of emotion unlike any Alexa had ever seen from her gruff and powerful father, he shoved the plate away, laid his head on the table, and wept.

Alexa sat and pulled her chair close to his, and put her arms around his powerful shoulders. He tried to gain control of himself, but it took him a few minutes of sniffling and heaving for him to stop and look up.

Once he did, he spoke plaintively to his daughter, as if to defend his failure—to apologize for it. "Duster and I went south and tried to pick up their trail. The path was dusty and we could make out the wheels of the cart for a mile or so. Then we came to a place where many roads intersected the path, and we couldn't pick up which way they'd gone. We picked one way, and upon finding a house, we asked whether anyone had seen a cart or the men we described. They hadn't, so we figured we'd picked the wrong direction. We traveled back to the fork and picked another direction. We did it two more times before night fell. Not a sign! No one we asked had seen them. It's like those bastards vanished into the air!"

"You'll find them, Dad," Alexa said. "It's better that you didn't catch up with them today anyway. Once Mr. Eckerly sends some of his men and you have a proper search party, you'll be a more dangerous force for those…men."

"Maybe, dear. Get me the wine bottle from the pantry," he said.

John didn't drink much. He only kept a bottle or two of red wine on the top shelf of the pantry, mainly for when guests visited.

When Alexa brought him the bottle, he pulled the cork and took a long swig. He raised it to Alexa. "You want some?"

Alexa took the bottle and let a little of the tart wine pass her lips. She didn't like the taste very much, but she liked the warm sensation in her throat and chest.

John stood up. "You've done well. Cleaning up the house and all. Tomorrow, we'll ask Mr. Eckerly to get the priest. We'll plan the funeral in the morning, and then hopefully we'll find those animals."

The next few days Alexa found herself very busy. Alexa,

John, and Michael walked through the fields to Mr. Eckerly's house the next morning. There, John went inside and spoke to Mr. Eckerly for a few minutes. Many of the farm hands came up to Alexa and Michael, while they waited outside, and offered their condolences, with promises to bring food to their home or to assist John in capturing and bringing the murderers to justice.

After that, they traveled to the north end of the farm to Bill Weldon's home. He was a craftsman who worked with various woods and metals, but when someone on the farm died, he carved headstones. Weldon had worked for Mr. Eckerly for more than twenty years, and every stone on the farm had been carved by him.

When they returned home they found a basket already on the porch. It was a small one, with one loaf of bread and some wild fruits and nuts in it. A small wooden box was wedged in the bottom of the basket. As Alexa opened it, she saw a small silver bracelet with a half-moon charm on it. The half-moon was a dark emerald. Inside was a note written on coarse paper.

Dear Mr. Flynn, Alexa, and Michael,

I am very sorry for your loss. Mrs. Flynn always showed me great kindness, and I will miss her very much. Please accept this bracelet as a proper adornment for her burial.

Yours in sorrow,
Duster

Alexa read the note over again. It was strikingly formal. It didn't sound like anything that Duster would write. Alexa brought both the box and the note to her father, who was sitting at the table with Michael. He read the note and looked at the bracelet.

"It's a fine piece. That's mighty generous of the boy," he said. He turned back to his son. "Michael, get me the wine bottle from the pantry."

Alexa slipped the box and the note into the pocket of her apron.

The next few days went by very quickly for Alexa. Her father had been allotted a few days and a few of the farm hands to track down the murderers and to bring them to Mr. Eckerly—for any crime done on his land was his to deal with. Alexa doubted that her father would have returned with the men. He probably would've killed them, but he never caught them.

While her father was absent, Michael stayed locked in his room most of the time. It was eerily silent, but twice, there was a sudden racket of furniture being moved around or something heavy slamming to the floor. Each time Alexa went to the door and asked Michael if everything was all right, he would bark at her to leave him alone.

Alexa was left to deal with the many visitors that Flynn House entertained in those days while her father was absent. Most of them were the men of the farm with their families. They brought what they could in the Flynns' time of need: bread, cakes, fruits, vegetables, bottles of wine and whiskey. Mr. Eckerly himself delivered a very generous basket, with two salted hams and a barrel of aged wheat beer that he brewed himself. Alexa graciously thanked her visitors, and assured them that her father and brother also sent their gratitude for the kindness they had been shown.

Four days after the murder, there was a small burial service overseen by the priest from the village to the north. It was early in the morning on a Tuesday. Alexa stood between her brother and father, dressed in a pale green gown of her mother's, while a man who had never met Miriam Flynn extolled her virtues and delivered her soul to eternal rest.

When the service was over, Michael and John gently lowered her body into the grave that John had dug just under the great tree to the west of their house. John picked up a clog of dirt and threw it into the grave, and walked slowly back to the house. Michael did the same. When it was Alexa's turn, she knelt and sprinkled the soft earth through her fingers onto the shroud that held her mother's body.

Alexa tried to stand, but her knees buckled as she was overcome with emotion. Suddenly a strong hand held her at the elbow. Alexa looked up into Duster's handsome face. He had been behind them the entire time, silently witnessing the service.

"Up you go," he said gently, and started to escort her to the house. She leaned heavily on him for the first two steps, and then regained her balance. As she took her first steps on her own, Duster said, "It was a lovely service."

Alexa shrugged. As Duster climbed the stairs before her, she thought about Duster having no one to hold him up after he had buried his own mother just a month earlier.

Duster opened the door for Alexa, and she nodded and went in. Duster followed her. Michael had evidently gone to his room. He was nowhere to be seen, but his bedroom door was closed and Alexa could hear him shuffling about behind it. John was seated at the table, a bottle of rye whiskey open before him.

He held up the bottle to Duster. "You're late for work, boy," he said roughly. "Mr. Eckerly is going to have your head."

"Mr. Eckerly gave me this morning to come to the service

49

and to do the job here, sir." Duster clasped his hands in front of himself, and then finding the posture awkward put his hands to his sides.

"Very generous of Mr. Eckerly and you." John took another swig from the bottle.

"Okay, Dad. That's quite enough for you this morning." Alexa grabbed at the bottle in his hand.

He pushed her hand roughly away from him. "Don't touch that." His voice was low and threatening. It had a note in it that Alexa had never heard before.

Alexa stopped where she was, shock distressing her pale features.

"Dad—" she began.

"Drop it!" he hissed.

Alexa turned away from him and went to the washbasin. She began scrubbing one of the large pots.

Duster silently watched this, holding his breath. When he finally released it, John looked up at him. "Haven't you got a job to do?"

Duster looked at Alexa's back and then at John. He nodded and went out to fill the grave.

Alexa scrubbed the pots and bowls, tears filling her eyes, but she did not turn around to face her father. She heard him take several more long drinks from the bottle and then he got up, knocking over his chair, and walked slowly into to his bedroom and shut the door.

When she was finished washing, Alexa went out the front door and walked across the grass to where Duster was filling the grave with earth. He'd rolled up the sleeves of a neatly kept work shirt, and he worked methodically, seeming to take perfect spadesful of dirt and place them gently in the grave. Alexa watched him for several minutes until he stopped to

50

stretch his back.

"Do you want some water?" she said to him.

"No thank you."

"I didn't put the bracelet on her," Alexa said.

"What?"

"Your mother's bracelet. I didn't put it on Mom before we buried her," Alexa said.

"Why not?" Duster looked angrily up at her. "Is there something wrong with my mother's bracelet?"

Alexa shook her head quickly. "No. It's not that. It's lovely."

"Then why wouldn't you put it on your mother? A woman should be buried properly—with proper jewelry and all." Duster squinted against the sunlight.

"She was. I made her a bracelet of twine with a wooden charm I carved in the shape of a half-moon," Alexa said.

"That's not right. How did your father allow that?" Duster said.

Alexa rolled her eyes. "In case you didn't notice, he's not really in any condition to examine things closely."

Duster looked up at the house, but didn't say anything. He still looked angry.

"We couldn't accept it, Duster. I figured that it was your mother's. She probably only had a couple of pieces of jewelry to begin with, and you buried her in one and gave the other to us. It belongs to you." With that, Alexa pulled up the sleeve of her dress, revealing the bracelet with the half-moon charm. She slipped it off of her wrist and held it out to Duster.

Duster looked at it for a moment. He looked up into Alexa's face. "You keep it," he said. Alexa opened her mouth to protest, but Duster cut her off before she began. "I have mother's books. I have the notes she wrote me. I have her house. I'll never forget her. A trinket like that should be worn by a woman, not kept in a box under an orphan's bed."

Alexa wrapped her fist around the bracelet. "I don't know what to say. Thank you, Duster. I'll cherish it always."

Duster nodded, but couldn't meet Alexa's eyes.

"There's something I've been meaning to ask you," Alexa said. "The note?"

"What about it?" Duster still wouldn't look up.

"It was very...formal." Alexa's voice betrayed her amusement at the last word.

Duster finally looked up and grinned. "Yeah. I didn't know what to write, so I found an old letter that someone had sent my mother when my grandmother passed away. I nearly copied it word for word."

Alexa laughed. "It didn't sound like you. It was very strange. You sounded like a professor or something." She curtsied and stiffened her upper lip as she lifted her head. "Excuse me, old chap, but am I properly adorned?"

Duster laughed loudly and returned a deep formal bow. "Why, of course, madam."

Fifty yards away, inside the house, Michael sat just beyond the light's reach before his bedroom window, watching Alexa and Duster beneath the great tree. As they bowed, he stood up and drew the curtains tightly closed, leaving himself in total darkness.

Then suddenly, a small circle of light appeared. It glowed brilliantly at the tip of Michael's index finger. Everywhere Michael moved his finger, the circle followed, leaving a fleeting trail of light. He closed his fist and the light disappeared.

CHAPTER 4
THE CALL

Three weeks later, Alexa found herself alone in the kitchen. Her father was at work in the fields, and Michael had once again risen early and left before either she or John had awoken. Alexa sat at the table with a wooden box. She lifted the lid gently and began to sort through the contents. There were letters and a few formal documents tied together with a piece of twine. There was a ruffled veil, as well as a small diary with yellowed pages.

Alexa looked at the veil. It was a simple country veil, but it was lovely, with fine lacework at the top. She imagined her mother, just a little older than herself, smiling through it as she rushed back up the aisle after marrying her father.

Alexa turned the packet of documents over in her hand, but did not untie them. They appeared to be land notices, probably a marriage license, and a few letters.

She opened the diary with great interest. It was her mother's, and from the date of the first entry, Alexa estimated that she must've been about thirteen when she began it. It was obvious that Miriam had only learned to write before starting the diary, and the first entries were about her own father, who had been injured by a horse on his farm, teaching her to write in the many months of his recovery.

Alexa read the diary for the next couple of hours. The entries were not regular. Miriam had written in it once every few weeks, and usually after some event of interest. She didn't have time to read the whole thing, so Alexa flipped through the pages of the diary looking for really important moments. Alexa read her mother's account of her own father's death, a large wild fire that consumed the fields of their estate, and her romance with John Flynn.

She couldn't help being moved by the description of their courtship, and how her father had been such a tender and romantic suitor, making her mother gifts and bringing flowers from the farthest corners of the county.

Alexa instinctively raised her head to look into her father's bedroom. She could see the empty bottle on the nightstand. Her father had already drunk everything the neighbors had brought him except for Mr. Eckerly's wheat ale, which he said tasted like dust, and had begun taking part of his wages in bottles.

Alexa replaced the contents of the box and put them back in her father's room. She then continued her morning work. She was kneading dough for their evening bread when Alexa heard the faint sounds of wheels coming up the path. Her muscles immediately tensed, as it reminded her of the squeaking of the murderers' cart as they drove leisurely toward her house that morning just a few weeks before.

She turned toward the window, but stood frozen with fear as she stared at the shutter, which was still closed in mourning. Alexa found her breath coming hard and fast, and she listened intently for the wheels to stop, which would tell her that the murderers had returned to finish the job.

Suddenly, the shutters flew open and Alexa could see out

onto the path. The cart, driven by old Cal Verner, who lived on the north end of the farm, wheeled past. Alexa finally felt her breathing relax, and released the vice grip she had on the edge of the kitchen table as she realized that the danger was only in her overwrought mind.

Then, she walked forward to examine the shutters. How had they opened like that? They had been latched shut. When she examined the latch it was broken, as if someone with great strength had pulled the shutters open from the outside, snapping the heavy latch like celery.

Alexa poked her head out the window, but there was no one there.

An hour before sundown, Michael came into the house. He was sweaty, and his face and hands were covered in dirt and grime, but he was stifling a smile.

"You're tracking mud in the house," Alexa said in a tone dangerously close to her mother's.

Michael stopped and looked up. He couldn't suppress the smile any longer. "Sorry." His white teeth shone brightly against his grimy features. He stood on one foot and reached down to pull off one of his boots.

"What are you so happy about?" Alexa said, placing plates on the table.

Michael stared at her for a moment. "You want to see?"

Alexa stopped setting the table and looked up at Michael. He raised his hands to the level of his chest, and suddenly, all three of the plates Alexa had just laid on the table rose into the air. Michael moved his hands in circles and they began to weave around each other. They looked like the balls being thrown by a juggler.

Alexa let out a scream of shock. Michael held his hands still and the plates stopped moving. He lowered his hands and the plates gently rested on the table.

"What was that?" Alexa said, pointing to the table.

"Magic," he whispered.

Alexa stood, dumbfounded, but then she thought about the day in the forest and how Michael's hand had burned her arm. She still had some discolored skin at the spot, even though the wound had healed well. Alexa had hundreds of words hurtling through her mind at that moment, but only one found its way to her lips. "How?"

Michael shook his head. "I don't know. I truly don't. I've been wondering about it since that day in the forest. I got angry and suddenly my hand burned your arm. Then it happened again, just a day later when I fought with the robber. I had my hands on his neck, and I was going to burn him through to the bone until he knocked me down. But I figured out that whenever I became angry, I mean truly angry, I had this power. I could make my hands burn like a fire, or I could make a small flame appear in the darkness. So I've been practicing. I've been going out into the forest, and at first, all I could do was make myself as angry as possible and then see what happened. But the more I did it, I realized that I could control what I was doing." Then, suddenly, Michael laughed. It was a wild, hysterical sound, more like shock than humor.

Alexa watched uncomfortably as Michael regained control of himself. Michael's chest heaved as if he could barely contain the energy within his body.

"Well, at least now you can't say you don't have a talent," Alexa said lightly.

Michael laughed another wild laugh, and strode into his room with the smile still on his face.

Alexa stood for a long while thinking about what Michael had told her. Magic. It didn't seem possible that her sulky, angry brother could really possess such power.

Dinner that night was the same as always. John came home sullen and weary. He ate little and went off to his room with a bottle. Michael went into his darkened room, and Alexa could occasionally see small flashes of light from under the door or hear furniture banging around. Before, she'd assumed that those sounds had been Michael angrily pushing around furniture in mourning. Now she knew that he was practicing.

Alexa cleaned up from dinner and went outside to wait for Duster. It was Alexa's favorite part of the day when he passed by in the evening. Not that she was happy that her father was drinking alone in his room, or that her brother was honing his new secret powers, but she was glad that there was little chance that they would be interrupted.

Alexa sat in the grass out front with her shoes off. The night was humid, but there was a soft breeze. Alexa stretched out on the grass, resting on her elbows as she kept her eyes on the path.

Like clockwork, she saw Duster's shadow appear on the path just a moment before he emerged from behind the hill. He walked slowly, but there was still a bouncing stride to his steps. As he approached, he stopped on the path in front of Alexa. "Evening," he said cheerily.

"Evening."

Duster took two steps off the path directly in front of Alexa and sat down. They sat only a few feet from each other. Neither of them said anything for a few minutes. They just sat listening to each other breathe.

"There's food inside if you're hungry," Alexa said.

She could see Duster shake his head in the moonlight. "No thanks. I've got stuff at home."

"You say that every time I ask," Alexa shot back. "I'm

beginning to think that you're afraid of my cooking."

Duster laughed. "It's not that."

"What is it, then?" Alexa asked, a little more forcefully than she'd meant to.

Duster sat thoughtfully for a moment. "It's just that I really like talking to you, and I'm not sure we'd be able to talk inside."

Alexa thought about her father, and how before he seemed to have been amused by Duster's interest in his daughter. She doubted that he would be so good-natured about it now.

"You're probably right," she said.

They sat in an awkward silence for a while. Finally, Duster spoke up. "So, you'll test for Bentham next month, huh?"

"No, actually," Alexa said. "The robbers took everything we had. Mr. Eckerly gave Dad a little advance on his pay, but it won't be enough. We can't afford for me to go to Bentham."

Duster tried to make out Alexa's expression in the darkness. "Are you angry about that?"

"Not really. Even if they hadn't taken all of our money, I wouldn't have gone anyway. Who would take care of the house? Of Dad?" Alexa picked at the grass blades in front of her.

"Your father is still a capable man. And…well, Michael is—" Duster started to say.

Alexa turned toward the house as she said, "Michael won't be here forever. And Dad isn't who he used to be. I don't know if he'll ever get back to himself."

"Where is Michael going?" Duster asked.

"I don't know. I just have a feeling—that's all."

Alexa was still watching the house, and she could see a tiny point of light from the window of Michael's room. It wasn't moving. Alexa had the distinct feeling that Michael was listening.

"So what about you?" Duster asked.

Alexa shrugged. "I'll probably begin working in the fields again for part of the day, and tend the house."

"For the rest of your life?" Duster's voice had a strange note in it.

Alexa's voice rose. "What? Are you judging me?"

"I don't get it, Alexa. You can't stay here. You're meant for something bigger than this. All the studying you've done? All of your talents? And you're going to waste away on this farm until some farm hand makes you his wife?"

"Was that a proposal?" Alexa's voice was still raised in anger, but there was a hint of confused humor in it.

Duster stood up. "Absolutely not. I wouldn't think of asking you to marry me."

Duster's words jolted Alexa. She stood up, too. Her fists were balled at her sides, and she was fighting to keep tears out of her eyes. "Fine," she shouted.

Duster lowered his voice until it was barely above a whisper. "Alexa, I'm going to die on this farm. I'm never going anywhere. There's no way I would let that happen to you."

Both Duster and Alexa stared hard at the shadow shape of the other just a few feet away. They said nothing for a long while.

Finally, Duster stepped back onto the path. "It's late. I should get going. Good night, Alexa," he said.

Duster walked on, leaving Alexa alone in the darkness.

The next morning, Michael emerged from his room as Alexa was preparing breakfast. "Morning," he said to her back.

She didn't respond.

Michael reached around Alexa to grab one of the biscuits she had baked. "What's the matter with you?"

"As if you don't know," she said without turning. "I know

59

you were listening last night."

"Oh…you and loverboy?" Michael chuckled.

"Shut up."

"He's right, you know," Michael said. "If you married him you'd be a laborer's wife. Is that what you want?"

Alexa slammed a bowl on the table. "I don't know what I want, okay? A month ago I was headed to Bentham, where I could make anything I wanted out of my future. And now… who knows what's going to happen?"

It was just then that a wail came from somewhere outside the house. Both Michael and Alexa turned toward the window. Alexa rushed toward it and looked out. There was nothing in front of the house, but the sound, a rushing melodic note, hung in the air. As Michael stepped behind her and looked over her shoulder, scarlet lightning flashed against the clear blue morning sky.

"Did you see that?" Alexa said, still staring out the window.

"Yes. It was like lightning, but there's not a cloud in the sky," Michael said, transfixed.

Alexa turned, pushed Michael out of the way, and ran out to the front of the house. Michael followed. They stood just before the path, listening to the sound and waiting for the strange sight to happen again. Alexa was sure it would.

As if in answer to her thoughts, the scarlet lightning appeared above the tree line of the woodland, just beyond the fields. Michael darted off in that direction, and after a moment of hesitation, Alexa followed him.

Michael headed toward the southern end of the woodland over which the lightning had appeared. Alexa was running her hardest, but Michael's long strides outpaced hers. Just before they reached the trees, the scarlet lightning flashed again.

They pushed on through the foliage toward where he

believed the sound and the signal were coming from. After a moment's confusion of the direction, Michael found himself at the edge of a clearing that he was certain that he'd never seen before. It was much larger than the area that had been cleared where their grove had once stood. In fact, this clearing was so large that there was a small wooden cottage in it.

As Alexa ran up from behind, Michael saw an old woman, hunched over, standing in front of it. The old woman was wrapped in a weathered white shawl and looked small, with thin wisps of stringy hair blowing around her head. Her mouth was open, and it seemed that the melodic wail was flowing from it. It was strange, because the sound didn't sound like it could be made by a human voice.

Suddenly, the strange woman put her hands toward the sky and the scarlet lightning flashed against the robin's egg blue. After she brought her hands down, she scanned the trees before her. Her eyes rested on Michael, who was standing with his hand on the trunk of a gray elm.

"I wondered how long I would wait for you," she said. "Come out, children."

Alexa had planted herself behind a tree to hide, but Michael stood out in the open, transfixed by the old woman and her power. He took one look at Alexa and then stepped forward.

"A fair young lad," the old woman said. After a moment, Alexa darted out from the wood and joined her brother. "And his careful sister," the old woman drawled.

"We're sorry to disturb you," Michael said.

"Disturb me? Nonsense! I was calling you," the old woman said, advancing toward them in halting, painful steps.

"Why is that? Alexa looked back at the wood, deciding whether or not to make a break for it.

"You needn't fear me, deary," the old woman said. "I am

Violet, and I'm here to give you a great gift."

"How did you make the lightning?" Michael asked. His eyes were slits.

"Magic," Violet said.

No one moved. Michael stared at the old woman with her high cheekbones and her eager eyes. Alexa looked from the old woman, to her brother, and back again.

"Can you teach me?" Michael said.

"Of course. That is why I have called you. This signal can only be seen by those who possess the power. I have been watching you two for a long time," Violet said. She came forward to within a few feet of them, and Michael and Alexa saw her slender frame and her bowed back. Violet's emerald eyes looked out from the leathery skin of her face.

"You've been watching the two of us? But she doesn't have the power," Michael said, waving a hand toward Alexa as he spoke.

"Oh yes, she does," said the old woman. "She has the same power coursing through her veins as you do, Michael Flynn. She just does not realize it yet."

"You're wrong," Alexa said. "I've never been able to do any sort of magic."

Violet had come directly before them now. She put a bony hand up to Alexa's face. "We shall see, my dear," she said. "However, there can be no doubt that you possess the power — you saw the lightning. Only a person who has this power could see it. Look around. Ask yourself why there are no others here. There should be, right? The sound was loud, and surely reached every corner of the Eckerly Farm. And you saw the lightning in the daylight sky. It was large and ominous, to be certain. And yet no one else has come to find out what strange happenings might be taking place. It is because you are the only ones who could see it."

Alexa and Michael both looked around. Violet seemed to be telling the truth.

"Can you teach me?" Michael asked again.

"Yes, Michael. I will teach you. I am old and not long for this world. Before I go, I look to help others realize their power," she said.

PATRICK IOVINELLI

CHAPTER 5
PROMISES AND POWER

"How do we begin?" Michael asked.

"Yes, you are eager," Violet said. She walked directly in front of Michael and put her hand up to his cheek. She brushed it gently. "You are young. You are strong. You will do well." As her bright eyes held Michael's, she seemed to recognize the interest and hope in them. She smiled softly, pressing even more wrinkles into her skin.

Then Violet stepped over to Alexa. She reached up and held Alexa's chin in her hand. Alexa could feel the calloused fingers pressing into her jawbone. She had to fight the urge to swat Violet's hand away. Violet's eyes danced like green flame. Alexa thought she sensed just the slightest amusement in those bright, dancing eyes.

As the old woman spoke, Alexa could see the gaps in her teeth and hear the hiss in her voice. "You are hard to read, my dear. I feel very little of the power emanating from you. There is much in its way. Your feelings, your studies, your desires — these will do nothing but tax your powers unnecessarily. If you are to learn how to use your power, you must dedicate yourself

64

to the study and practice of it above all other things—above all other people."

Alexa caught a knowing look in Violet's eyes as she said these last words. Alexa pulled her chin out of Violet's grasp. The old woman let out a creaking wheeze. Alexa realized it must have been a laugh.

"What am I to do?" Michael asked.

Violet took two steps back and faced them. "You will come tonight at midnight. Then I will begin your training. But first, you must promise to tell no one of your magic. All around there are people who are stupid and fearful of our power. We must avoid them and try not to arouse their suspicions. You must not even tell your father," she said.

"Why not?" Alexa said.

"He lacks vision," the old woman hissed.

"Fine. We will tell no one," Michael answered promptly.

"Hey, you don't speak for me," Alexa said.

"This is the only choice," Violet said. "You must decide."

Alexa could feel every hair on the back of her neck standing. All she wanted to do was run away from this place and this strange woman.

Then Michael put his hand on her shoulder. "Come on, Alexa."

She looked up into Michael's eyes and saw fear, but it wasn't a fear of this stranger or her promises. It was the fear of a hopeless future on the farm. Alexa had seen it in his eyes for months.

"Fine," she said, looking at Michael.

Violet clapped. "Excellent. We begin tonight, children."

Michael and Alexa walked home slowly. Alexa kept glancing furtively at Michael. He took slow, plodding steps, as if he were in a trance. Alexa imagined that Michael was dreamily thinking about what spells and powers Violet would teach him.

Alexa, however, was worried. There was just something in the gleam of Violet's bright eyes that she didn't trust. However, if she and Michael really had these powers, there was no choice — they had to learn how to use them.

When they reached the house, Alexa went in expecting to see her father at the breakfast table, but he wasn't there.

She walked to his room and opened the door. Her father was snoring heavily in his bed. Alexa went in and opened the shutters. He still didn't stir, so she went to him.

"Dad. Dad, come on. It's time to get up for work," she said, shaking him gently.

"I'm not going out there today. Tell Eckerly I'm sick," he muttered, and turned over in the bed.

"Dad, are you all right? Does something hurt you?" Alexa tried to turn him back toward her.

Suddenly, John rolled toward her. "Alexa! Do as I say. I'm not going out into the fields today. Now leave me alone!" he yelled. His face was red under his scraggly whiskers and his eyes were puffy. Alexa could still smell the whiskey on his breath. He flung her hand off his shoulder. "Now get out!" he screamed, and turned away.

Alexa went back out into the kitchen and closed the door behind her.

Michael was still in the kitchen. "What was that about?"

"I don't know," Alexa said. "I've never seen him like that."

"It's best to let him alone," Michael said. "Maybe he'll be better after a few more hours of sleep."

But Michael was wrong. John slept until late in the morning, but was in an even worse mood when he woke up. Michael had gone a few hours earlier, so Alexa was alone when her father came out of his room and sat unsteadily at the table.

Alexa quickly brought tea, biscuits, and even some of the ham left over from the previous night's dinner. John ate ravenously, but silently. The only sound to be heard was his knife banging off the plate.

Alexa stood at the washbasin and kept her back to him. When he was done, he heaved the plate into the middle of the table, walked over to the washbasin, shoved Alexa out of the way, and rubbed some water on his face.

"Dad," Alexa said timidly.

"What?" he barked.

"I was thinking that maybe I should start working in the fields in the morning with you, to help us out. I'd work half the day, and then come home to do my chores and make dinner," she said.

He turned and looked down at her. "Do whatever you want," he said, wiping the water from his eyes with a towel. He tossed it on the table and went back to his room. He slammed the door behind him.

Alexa stood in shock and then ran out of the house. She stood in front of the house for a moment, trying to figure out where to go. Alexa had to get away, but she didn't want to head toward the grove because she was fairly certain that Michael would be there. And she didn't want to head toward the fields because she didn't want to see any of the other farmhands.

Alexa darted past the great tree, under which her mother was buried, and headed west toward the river, sprinting the whole way. She finally stopped before the rippling water. Her chest was on fire and her head was swimming. Alexa bent at the waist and put her hands on her knees, trying to catch her breath, trying to make sense of it all.

Finally, she stood upright and screamed wildly across the water. The scream was harsh, grating, and it hurt her throat.

Alexa forced it out and pushed with all the air in her lungs until she couldn't breathe, and then she bent over once more.

The sound echoed over the water and into the woods beyond. When the echo died, Alexa could only hear the wind and the water.

As she stood upright again and turned back, she didn't know what to do. Alexa found herself staggering, without any idea where she was or where she was headed. Her footsteps dragged heavily, and she heard nothing as she raged through the fields.

Then, out of the corner of her eye, Alexa caught the slightest twitch of movement, and it brought her focus back to her surroundings. She was in a field of tall wheat. Alexa didn't know what else to do, so she ducked down. Suddenly, out of the wheat came an enormous man, larger than any man she had ever seen. He towered over her and had a broad, muscular frame — Alexa could tell even through his tunic. Alexa looked up and saw the man's helmet first. It was a battered, dented helm, with serpent's eyes etched on the front of it.

Then Alexa looked down from the helmet and into the man's face. He had a cruel face, with a brutal scar running down the left side, and wild, gray eyes. His skin was grimy, like it was covered in soot, but he had a neatly kept black beard.

The man stopped and looked down at Alexa. He made a huff, and in a moment was stalking off through the wheat in the other direction. Alexa dared to lift her head to watch him walk away, and she saw that he had a battle-axe strapped to his back. It was heavily notched.

Alexa knew better, but she was so curious about the large stranger that she popped up and began to walk after him. He was walking quickly and with great purpose through the wheat fields of Mr. Eckerly's farm. He was well ahead of her, but Alexa didn't mind that much. The man was stalking so rapidly she could tell where he was from the sound, and she didn't want to follow him too closely anyway.

As they neared the edge of the fields, Alexa heard the man's steps stop. She immediately stopped and held her breath, listening. Nothing.

She stood there for another half a minute, waiting to hear the steps continue, but they didn't. Then suddenly, the wheat parted to her left and the man was on her. The battle-axe was in his hands and he held it high over his head. There was nothing for Alexa to do. She dropped to the ground and flung her arms over her head.

Alexa heard the whoosh of the axe coming down, but the blow never fell. There was the sound of a heavy clash of metal from above her head. Alexa waited a beat and then looked up. The big man was lying on his back, twenty feet away. Alexa only had a clear view because all the wheat between them had been knocked down.

The huge man was stunned. He flailed about for a moment, and then pushed himself up. His battle-axe was on the ground next to Alexa.

"How did you do that?" he said. His voice was a hoarse growl.

"I didn't do anything," Alexa said, still on her knees in the grass.

"Why are you following me?" he barked.

"Who are you, and what are you doing on Mr. Eckerly's farm?" Alexa said, pushing herself to her feet.

The big man laughed a booming, mirthless laugh. "Mr. Eckerly's farm? This is my land. I have what you might call a prior claim, little girl."

"Who are you?" Alexa repeated the question.

"Don't follow me," was all he said. With that, the man walked toward her and picked up his axe. He glared at Alexa, and she shrunk with fear under his gaze. His eyes were burning and bloodshot. The man slung the weapon across his back and bounded off toward the forest.

Alexa sat very still for a while and listened to the stranger crash through the brush. Alexa couldn't explain it, but the fear she felt when she looked into those horrible red eyes drove her to get away — but she couldn't. She had to know who this mysterious stranger was and why he was on the farm, so she finally got up and crept along, heading in the direction of the forest and listening for the sound of the huge warrior. After a few minutes she could see his huge shape at the edge of the wheat fields, and it looked like he was headed right for the grove.

Alexa kept her distance but continued to follow. As they approached the grove, Alexa heard voices and crept silently along, until she finally planted herself behind a fallen tree just outside of it. She peeked through the trees.

Seated on the stumps that were in a semicircle were the strangest people Alexa had ever seen. On the stump the farthest to the left sat a thin, sickly looking man with a whispering voice, and the most horrible sores covering his face and hands. Next to him was a woman. Even though she was seated, she appeared to be tall and powerful. Her bare arms were lined with muscles, and her hair was wild, vivid red. It seemed to blow around in all directions even though there wasn't a wind today. The third seat was occupied by a handsome man dressed in neat, cerulean robes. This man had wise, dark eyes and a sneering lip. The gigantic warrior with the battle-axe took the last stump.

They all sat talking quietly until out from the woods walked a little girl. The girl looked to be about ten, with golden hair.

The girl's pale features were sharp, but her cheeks were just the slightest shade of pink. Once Alexa saw the little girl, she couldn't look away from her. The others fell silent at the sight of her.

The little girl sat on the stump that faced the others and said, "We are not alone." At that, the other four jumped to their feet and started to scan the area. Alexa dove back behind her log.

"Be seated," Alexa heard the little girl say.

Alexa dared to peek over the log. The first three had already resumed their seats. The warrior was still standing and peering around the clearing. He didn't seem to notice Alexa.

The little girl looked at the warrior. "Caelan."

The warrior turned back toward the little girl and sat begrudgingly. "I know who it is — " he began.

"It is of no consequence," the little girl cut him off.

The warrior bristled, but fell silent.

"Caelan, you know why we are here. This land faces a threat — an unnatural threat. Our charge is to enforce the laws of nature above all else. I know it angers you to see your fields filled with farmers instead of soldiers — to see the horizon blazing with the brilliant sunset rather than the fires of war. But these people have done nothing to deserve your enmity. There is only one thing that threatens our law here. That is all we shall deal with. Nothing else."

Although her voice was that of a child, Alexa heard a firmness, a strength in the voice of the little girl that she had never heard before. The giant warrior seemed to sense it, too. He bowed his head in deference.

"There may be a time for each of you to play your part in this, but it is not now. We must wait until the threat makes itself known, and wait for these people to meet it," she said.

71

"They are weaklings," the warrior muttered.

The handsome man next to him nodded. "You are right, Caelan. But we can do nothing yet."

The little man covered in sores coughed. "I daresay you will have a hand to play in this before it is over, Breg."

The man next to Caelan nodded again. He smoothed the front of his robes absentmindedly, and returned his attention to the little girl.

"None of you is to interfere with the events about to unfold. Only when the laws of nature are threatened will we come forward." The little girl's eyes fell on each of the people sitting before her. They lingered for a moment on the warrior.

Silently, the little girl rose and turned to head back into the trees. Alexa realized that once the little girl was gone, Caelan might start looking for her again. She crawled quickly and silently along the ground until she felt it was safe to stand. She got up and without looking back, she ran all the way home.

An hour later, Alexa stood in the doorway of Michael's room, whispering to him what she had seen in the forest.

"Who were they?" Michael asked.

"I have no idea. They looked like some sort of council, but why would a little girl be at the head? And why would they meet out in a forest?" Alexa said.

"They must have been the ones who cleared the trees," Michael said.

"They must have," Alexa agreed.

Michael's eyebrows were furrowed in concentration. "Maybe we should ask Violet about them?"

"I don't know, Michael."

"Why not? Maybe she knows who they are and why they're here," he said.

Alexa thought for a moment. She didn't know why, but

Alexa didn't want to tell Violet about this strange woodland council.

"Didn't Violet warn us not to 'tax our powers'? Didn't she tell us that to study magic would require focus?" Alexa said.

Alexa could tell that Michael wasn't sure, but that he certainly didn't want to jeopardize his opportunity to learn from Violet.

"Maybe you're right. Maybe we won't mention it yet," he said.

Alexa moved about the kitchen, preparing dinner, but her mind was on the council. She just couldn't imagine who they were and what kind of "unnatural threat" they had been talking about.

When she'd finally finished setting out the plates, she went to her father's room and knocked on the door.

"Go away." Her father's voice strained through the door.

"Dad, you have to eat."

"Not now, Alexa." There was weariness in her father's voice that struck Alexa. All the anger he'd taken out on her earlier seemed to have left him. The voice that came through the door was small, broken. Alexa walked away from the door and went over to Michael's room.

She knocked. "Dinner."

Michael came out and looked at John's empty seat at the table. "Where's Dad?"

"He doesn't want to eat," Alexa said.

Michael then picked up his plate and began to carry it off toward his room.

"Michael," Alexa pleaded.

"I've got to practice before tonight. You should, too," he said.

"I have nothing to practice," Alexa said, but Michael was

already gone.

Alexa sat at the table alone. She picked half-heartedly at her food, but didn't eat much.

Just before midnight, Michael and Alexa set out from their house into the forest. They found the large clearing and peered anxiously through the trees to see Violet's cottage. It was there on the far side, illuminated by the pale moon. Violet stood before it, swaying slightly in the breeze, a walking stick clutched in her left hand.

"Good evening, children," Violet said.

"Good evening," Michael answered.

Violet turned her face slowly toward Alexa, who was trudging up slowly behind her brother. Violet held her gaze on Alexa until she finally muttered, "Evening."

"Very good, children. We must first assess your powers. Michael, you will go first."

Michael nodded and stepped forward. He balled his hands into fists and then stretched them convulsively as he stood before Violet. Alexa stood back and watched quietly.

Violet stared up into Michael's face. The tiniest hint of a sneer appeared as she spoke. "What brings forth your power?"

"Anger," Michael said. His voice echoed unnaturally in the clearing.

"Yes. Good. Very good," Violet said. "Show me."

Michael screwed up his face in concentration and started to take short, fierce breaths. Suddenly, Michael brought his fingertips together and they glowed an incandescent orange. Michael closed his eyes to keep his concentration.

"Release it," Violet said.

Michael opened his eyes. "How?" he asked.

Violet smiled, showing a gap in her teeth. The pale moon made her haggard face look sinister. "Push it toward your

74

enemy," she said.

Michael turned to his right and squared himself to a tree that stood off at the edge of the clearing. Suddenly, his fingers broke apart as he thrust his palms forward. The glow hurtled from Michael's hand and hit the tree. Its heavy trunk split, and one side of the tree fell to the ground.

"Magic is energy," Violet said.

Michael gaped at the tree trunk he'd just split. "What?" he said.

"It is pure energy," Violet said. "If a person possesses the power, he can call it forth when he is in the proper state of emotion. In your life, Michael, you have been frustrated, mistreated...an afterthought."

"Yes," Michael said, his eyes flashing.

"So naturally," Violet continued, "your power rises when you are frustrated and angry. Up to now, you've probably found yourself making wondrous things happen when you were angry, but with no way to explain them."

"I don't know about 'wondrous,'" Alexa said, rubbing her arm where she could still feel the newly formed skin that had covered the burn.

Violet continued as if she'd heard nothing. "It is only through the study of magic spells that we can bend this energy to our will — to do specific things when we want. Otherwise, we would just continue to release our unbridled energy without form or purpose."

Michael stared at her.

"Step back," she said.

Michael looked down, hesitant, but obediently took two steps back and looked toward Alexa.

"Come forward, my dear," Violet said.

Alexa stepped before the old witch and stood at attention.

"What brings forth your power?"

Alexa held out her palms. "I already told you...I don't have any power," she said.

Violet took a step toward Alexa and peered keenly into her face. "Are you weak, my dear?"

"Weak?"

"Yes. Is your power stunted because you are weak and selfish, concerned only for your books and the smiles of farm boys?" Violet reached down and brushed the half-moon bracelet that hung on Alexa's wrist.

Alexa's ears reddened in anger. "I'm not weak," she said.

"Then show me your power," Violet said, taking a step back.

"I already told you—" Alexa began.

Violet cut her off. "Enough."

Alexa fell silent, but glared at the old woman. They stared at each other for a long moment. Finally, Violet said, "Perhaps your power comes from another state of emotion. We will have to test you and see."

Violet turned on her heel and walked slowly away toward her cabin. Her hood came down and Alexa noticed the top of a jagged, red cut high on Violet's shoulder. It looked fresh, and almost reached the base of the old woman's neck. Alexa wondered what could possibly have made such a terrible wound. Alexa stared intently at it as the old woman walked away.

It wasn't until Violet had almost reached the shadows cast by her small cottage that Alexa realized that someone was standing in the doorway of it. The person had a slight, familiar shape, but it was too dark for Alexa to tell who it was.

"Who's there?" Alexa called.

The person walked out of the doorway with a slow, rhythmic

gait. As the pale moon illuminated the woman's features, Alexa saw the soft oval of her mother's face.

Alexa breathed sharply and put her hand to her mouth. After a moment's hesitation she ran wildly toward her mother, who continued to come forward. As Alexa ran, she opened her arms to put her mother in a clutching embrace, but as Alexa reached her, the illusion vanished, and Alexa landed hard on the ground.

Violet's soft, wheezing laughter registered in her ears.

Alexa scrambled to her feet. "Bring her back," she said into the darkness where she heard the laughter.

"I cannot but recall her image from your haunted mind," Violet said. "But you...her daughter...her favorite...you can bring her back from death to life."

Alexa looked into the darkness toward where Violet was standing, and then back toward the place where the vision of her mother had appeared. "No. That's impossible. Nothing can bring back the dead," Alexa said.

Violet stepped forward into the light of the pale moon and stared at Alexa. "We shall see."

Michael, who had been holding his breath, rushed forward. "How? How can we do it?" he demanded.

"You cannot do it, Michael," Violet said flatly. "Only *she* can do it."

Michael stomped over to Alexa and grabbed her by the arm; she felt the flesh about to burn and shrugged him off. She looked down at her arm, but there was nothing there.

"Alexa, you have to do it," he said. Michael leaned over her, and his eyes glinted in the pale moonlight.

Alexa drew herself up to her full height and stared back at Michael. "I don't have to do anything. And anyway, I can't," she said. "Even if I wanted to...I don't know how."

Michael looked away from her, and then Alexa turned to look at Violet. There was a flicker of a smile on Violet's lips that was quickly extinguished.

"Perhaps you do not possess the power after all," Violet said. Her face was stony, but Alexa could detect a hint of malice in the hissing words.

"Fine." Alexa stormed away through the clearing and into the forest.

"Alexa! Alexa!" Michael yelled.

Alexa heard his footsteps as he started to jog after her, but then she heard Violet's hissing murmur again. But it was not loud enough for Alexa to hear what she said.

Michael's footsteps stopped abruptly.

With tears streaming down her face, Alexa raced through the woods. She didn't stop even though the stitch in her side urged her to.

She finally stopped when her dark house came into view. Breathing raggedly, she walked slowly back through the night toward her home. There was no light in any of the windows. There was no smoke billowing from the chimney. The house was cold and forbidding in the pale moonlight.

Alexa walked up the steps and stopped in front of the green door. She opened it, but then shut it again. Alexa walked heavily down the steps and toward the tree that hung above her mother's grave.

Alexa sat down against the trunk, feeling its rough bark against her back. She folded her arms against the chill and closed her eyes; the soft light of the pale moon still lingered before her.

She reached up and wiped the tears from her cheeks. She thought of Michael, alone in the darkness with Violet; she thought of her father, passed out in his bed with a bottle; she thought of her mother, her careworn face shining with tears as she came forward to embrace Alexa.

Alexa turned her head and let her weariness overcome her. Then she slept.

CHAPTER 6
HOME FIRES

Alexa woke suddenly, alarmed by the sounds of footsteps nearby. She opened her eyes and took in the broad figure of her father walking unsteadily toward her. She heard concern in his gruff baritone.

"What are you doing out here? Are you all right?" Alexa thought he almost sounded like he used to, before Miriam had died. Even so, she refused to look at him.

"I slept out here," Alexa said, getting to her feet.

"Why would you do that?" John asked.

"What do you care?" she said, and made to walk past him. Alexa braced herself. She knew that he would reach out and grab her and scream at her for her insolence. But he didn't. He turned and watched her walked past him, up the steps, and into the house.

She went in and began preparing breakfast. John came in while she was working. He stood in the doorway for a few moments, watching her. Then he slowly came forward into the kitchen, and as she walked toward the basin, he touched her arm gently.

"Alexa," he said.

She didn't respond. She kept moving about the kitchen. John lowered his head and went back into his room, shutting the door behind him.

Alexa stalked toward Michael's room and pushed the door open. Michael was asleep on his back, fully clothed, snoring loudly. His mouth was open.

Alexa slammed the door and stomped back into the kitchen. She finished making breakfast and left the plates on the table for Michael and her father.

She stood back for a moment, and looked from Michael's door to her father's. Then she turned abruptly and walked out of the house. She marched up the path toward the Eckerly farm, rubbing her arms against the cool morning.

As she reached the fields where men were working, a few of them waved to her and she waved back listlessly. She didn't slow down until she heard someone call her name. She turned to see Duster carrying his shoes in one hand, coming up the path.

"What are you doing out here?" he asked when he'd caught up with her.

"I need to speak to Mr. Eckerly," Alexa said, walking away.

Duster reached out to take her arm. "Hold on —"

She jerked away from him and turned to face him. "What do you want, Duster?"

Alexa folded her arms and leaned on one foot, the picture of impatience. The look of shock on Duster's face would normally have made Alexa laugh, but she wasn't in the mood to laugh now.

"Can I walk with you?" he said.

She turned and continued up the path. "If you want."

Alexa refused to look at Duster the rest of the way, but she

81

could feel him staring at her.

"Are you all right?" he asked.

"Fine."

"Obviously," he said.

When they reached the fields in the center of the farm, Duster said, "Mr. Eckerly will probably be around the barn. He's been having a hard time with the animals now that your father has stopped coming to work."

Alexa stopped and looked at Duster. For the briefest moment, she felt like she might relax and talk to him normally, but she just couldn't.

"Thank you," was all she said, and walked away.

Duster watched her go. He opened his mouth to call after her, but stopped. He finally turned to head into the fields to the west.

Just as Duster had said, Alexa found Mr. Eckerly pouring slop into the trough for the pigs. He was muttering to himself.

"Excuse me, Mr. Eckerly," Alexa said.

He turned to look at her. He put down the slop pail and took a step toward her. "Yes, Alexa? Let me guess, your father is too ill to work again today?" he said icily.

"I have no idea whether or not he'll come to work today," she said. "But I know that someone must do his job, and I'm here to do it."

Mr. Eckerly chuckled and his forehead creased right above the eyebrows. "Are you serious?"

"Yes," Alexa said. "I worked in the fields until two years ago, if you remember. Perhaps now I can take over my father's duties here with the animals in the mornings?"

Mr. Eckerly looked at her skeptically.

"At least then, you wouldn't have to do it, sir," she said.

And that, of course, decided him. He nodded slowly and

handed the pail to Alexa. He was still staring at her as she took the pail and turned to walk away. "Do you want me to show you what to do?" Mr. Eckerly asked.

"I've got it," Alexa called over her shoulder.

Alexa found that she didn't need much reminding about what to do. She had helped her father tend the animals a lot when she was small, and the routine of it came back to her very quickly. Since Mr. Eckerly had already fed the pigs, she went around to the barn and made sure there was feed for the cows. She slowly bent under the gate and slid into the corral. There were three cows in there. The largest one turned in her direction, but didn't fret.

Alexa slowly reached down to feel her udder. She needed to be milked. It was common for the hands to milk the largest cow first, so if this one hadn't been milked, the other two needed it as well.

Milking the cows, as well as tending to the two goats and Mr. Eckerly's small chicken brood, took up most of Alexa's morning. Once she had finished, she found Mr. Eckerly walking through the barn, looking at the animals. Alexa had a feeling that Mr. Eckerly was checking her work.

Alexa approached him from behind. "Well?" she said.

Mr. Eckerly turned. "Well what?"

"How did I do? Did I forget anything?" Alexa asked.

"No. I believe you did everything your father should've done," he said, and walked away.

Alexa began the short trek through the fields to get to the path home. She saw men in the west fields clearing the wheat. She looked for Duster among them, but didn't see him.

She continued on the path under the afternoon sun. Beads of sweat made their way down her forehead as she squinted against the sunlight. Alexa was recounting all the chores she would have to complete this afternoon when she came around a bend and their small house came into view. She saw smoke rising, but not from the chimney — it was coming from one of the windows.

Alexa ran around to the side of the house and saw the blaze through Michael's bedroom window.

She ran back toward the front of the house, and just as she was about to climb the stairs to go in and make sure that Michael and her father were not in there, the door burst open and Michael stumbled out, pulling John behind him. Once they came into the open, Michael began to take great gulps of air in between coughs. He walked all the way up to the path and fell to his knees.

John turned on the porch and stared back into the house. His face was blackened from the soot, but there were clear streaks down his cheeks from his tears. Suddenly John rushed back inside.

Alexa screamed, "Dad!" and ran up the stairs after him. Taking a deep breath as she reached the last step, she darted into the house.

It was dark and the heat was unbearable. Alexa tried to swat away some of the smoke so she could see better, but she couldn't. She struggled toward Michael's bedroom and found that the fire was still contained within, but her father wasn't in there. She stumbled through the kitchen and found her father face down on the floor of his bedroom. At first Alexa thought he had passed out, but then she saw his arms scrambling under the bed. He was pulling the box of papers and keepsakes out.

When John saw Alexa, he pointed roughly at the front door. She nodded and turned to leave, but tripped in the kitchen. As she fell to her hands and knees, she began to crawl forward. Alexa suddenly felt John's hand on the back of her work shirt.

He set her upright and shoved her forward.

Alexa was blinded by the sunlight as she emerged from the house. She took one breath and then began to cough. She turned around to see Michael lying in the grass near the front steps.

John Flynn emerged from the door and walked slowly down the steps, the box in his arms. "Michael, are you all right?" he said. Michael sat up and nodded. John came over and patted him roughly on the head.

Michael started to get to his feet. "I'm fine," he said. He was still breathing heavily.

John said, "Then run down into the fields and find some of the men with a cart. Tell them to meet us by the river with pails and anything that can carry water."

Michael nodded and ran up the path.

John turned to look at Alexa, who was still sitting in the grass staring at her father. He walked over to her and held out his hands. "C'mon. We have to get water," he said.

Alexa nodded and let him pull her up. She ran around to the back and found two buckets near the back door. She could still hear the crackling flames inside the house. When she came back around, John had a large tub in his arms.

"Let's go," he said.

They walked in silence toward the river. They knew they had to go quickly, but they were both exhausted. Alexa didn't look up at her father until they reached the river. He bent over the water with the washing tub and let it fill. He struggled to pull it up without spilling.

Alexa bent down and held one of the buckets under the water. The cool water splashing on her arms and her neck felt wonderful in the oppressive heat.

She pulled the bucket back up and put it on the ground; Alexa reached for the other at the same time as her father. They both stopped and looked at each other.

Even with his face covered in soot, Alexa couldn't help noticing how handsome his face was. There were lines from the sun, but John's face was lively and full, accentuated by the brown beard that was almost black now because of the fire.

"That was a very brave thing you just did," he said. His voice broke at the last words and he looked away from her.

Alexa came forward and hugged him fiercely. "Oh, Dad. I was so scared. I thought you went in there to kill yourself," she said. She buried her face in his shoulder and sobbed.

John held her gently. He patted her hair like he used to when she was a little girl. "I know you did," he whispered.

They didn't speak at all until they heard the sounds of horses and creaking wheels approaching. Duster was driving a cart full of men, who carried pails, tubs—one even had a washbasin.

"Are you all right, Mr. Flynn?" Duster said as he jumped down and ran toward them. Duster stopped a few feet from them and looked down at Alexa, sobbing into John's shoulder. "Is she—?"

John nodded over Alexa's head and beckoned Duster toward him. He turned Alexa from him. "Stay with Duster," John said as he placed her in Duster's arms. "I've gotta go see if we can stop this fire."

Duster awkwardly put his arms around her and patted her on the back.

Alexa didn't even realize what had happened until the cart had pulled away, leaving her and Duster standing alone at the river. She suddenly lifted her head away from his shoulder and tried to pull away.

Duster didn't let go at first and peered down into her face. "Are you sure you're all right?"

Alexa nodded and wiped her eyes. Duster released her. He stood watching her as she took deep breaths and stared at the ground.

When she finally started to breathe a little easier, Duster spoke. "What happened?"

"I don't know. I came back from working in the barnyard and our house was on fire. I think it started in Michael's room, but I don't know. Dad and Michael came stumbling out of the house."

When she looked up at him, Duster looked perplexed. "I don't understand. You're covered in soot. Did you go into the house?"

Alexa looked down. "Yes. I wanted to get some of my books, but there wasn't time," she said.

Alexa could feel Duster staring at her. She was sure he knew she was lying, but he didn't press it. "Let's get back to your house and see if they need more help," he said.

Alexa nodded and walked slowly. Duster slowed his normal loping stride so that they could walk together.

By the time they reached the house, the fire was out. Most of the men were standing around outside the house, surveying the damage. John Flynn was standing near Michael's window, inspecting the blackened timbers.

Michael was standing at the front door, swinging it back and forth to fan some of the smoke out of the house. He turned and saw Alexa standing at the bottom of the stairs, and quickly turned away from her. Alexa stared at his back for a moment, and it suddenly dawned on her that the fire had started in Michael's room. He had been using his magic, and he'd almost burned the house down with their father in it.

Alexa suddenly felt like rushing up the stairs and slapping Michael across the face, but she couldn't do that in front of her father, Duster, or the other men. She narrowed her eyes and didn't look away from him, even as everyone else turned to look at the path as they heard more horses approaching.

Mr. Eckerly and two of the other farmhands rode up. Mr. Eckerly dismounted, surveying the burned house.

"Everyone survive?" he yelled across to John.

John nodded.

Mr. Eckerly walked slowly over near John, his eyes still taking in the burned timbers and soot-covered brick of the house. "How did it start?"

Alexa was still staring at Michael. He shifted from one foot to the other, but didn't look up.

John continued to look at the house, but made no reply.

Mr. Eckerly raised his voice so that all the men could hear. "Well? What happened? Were you drunk and knocked over a candle, or did you fall into the hearth spraying sparks on the rug? What was it?"

John sighed and turned toward Mr. Eckerly. "Yeah. That must've been it," he said.

"I've been very patient, John," he said. "I've been very understanding since Miriam, but this can't continue. I will not continue to pay you and allow you to live on my land—"

John cut him off. "I know, Mr. Eckerly. I'm sorry. It won't happen again," he said. "I'll be at work tomorrow."

Mr. Eckerly looked as if he wanted to say more to John, but he didn't. Wordlessly, he mounted his horse and rode back toward the center of the farm.

At this point, many of the men began to disperse and head back to work, realizing that Mr. Eckerly would be angry with further disruption of his farm's normal business. Some of the men came up to John and offered to help him clear the burned section of the house and rebuild it in the fall, when work hours were shorter.

John shook hands with some of them and thanked them as they left.

Alexa, Michael, and Duster hadn't moved since Mr. Eckerly had arrived.

Finally, after the last man left, Duster came forward. "Mr. Flynn, I can stay and help you—"

"No, Duster. Thank you, but you should go back to work. Mr. Eckerly will be angry if you stay here to help us." Duster opened his mouth to protest, but John put his hand on Duster's shoulder. "I appreciate it. I really do, but go," he said.

Duster looked up at Michael and then over at Alexa. "I'm glad everyone is okay, Mr. Flynn," he said.

"Me too, Duster. I'll see you tomorrow," and John put out his hand. Duster looked down at it and hesitated. Then he shook it.

Alexa and John watched Duster walk up the path back toward the farm. Michael still had his back turned.

John slowly walked around to the front of the house and climbed the steps. Michael moved to the side to let him pass, but didn't look up. John went in the house and came out a few moments later with his axe in its leather wrapping.

"Your room is a mess, Michael. I'm going to have to knock it down, and then we can get new timbers and rebuild it. There's only a little bit of damage to the kitchen." John turned. "Alexa, your room is fine. I wonder what happened."

Alexa couldn't hold it in any longer. She pointed at Michael's back. "It was him!"

"What?" John turned to look at Michael, who looked like he might take off running.

"Dad, he can do magic! He's been learning how to create fire with it. He was practicing in his room. That's how the fire started, isn't it?" she said to Michael's back.

Michael turned to face her. "Violet was right about you. You are weak…and scared!" he said

"What are you two talking about?" John looked back and forth several times, waiting for an answer, but it didn't come.

"There's no need to rebuild my room, Father," Michael said, his eyes on Alexa. "I'm leaving." Michael started down the steps.

"What do you mean?" John reached out to grab him, but Michael twisted to avoid his grasp. Michael ran down the steps, and bumped hard into Alexa as he passed her and ran up the path.

John stood near the doorway and watched Michael disappear around the bend, and then looked down at Alexa. "What is going on?"

Alexa put her head down and sighed.

Then she told him. She told him everything.

She told him about how Michael had burned her arm and the neck of one of the robbers. She told him about being called to Violet and their lessons. She told him about not being able to do any magic herself, even though Violet insisted that she must have the power because she could see the lightning.

John stood in silence for a long while. Even after Alexa finished he stood, and Alexa could tell he was trying to make sense out of this unbelievable story that she had just told him.

Alexa came forward and sat down on the bottom step. After a few moments, John came and sat next to her. He tossed the axe into the grass.

"I must really have been out of it not to notice that we had a magician in the house, huh?" he said.

Alexa looked over at him. "So you believe me?"

"Of course I believe you," he said. He opened his mouth to

90

say something else, but stopped.

"What is it, Dad?"

"Your mother made things happen—strange things that she couldn't explain."

"What?"

"I can show you," John said. He got up and walked over to where he'd left the small box of papers and keepsakes, and went through it until he came to Miriam's diary. Once he found it, he rifled through the pages until he found what he was looking for.

He held the book out to Alexa. "She said this happened when she was about seventeen, just a few months before we were married."

Alexa took the book and read the entry.

John came this morning and brought me daffodils from the Harkers' meadow. They were lovely. We sat in the grass behind the house, eating bread and laughing before we went to work.

I was sent home in the middle of the day to fetch some rivets Father needed for his leatherworking. As I approached the house, I saw a wiry thief skulking beneath the window. I knew Mother was alone with the baby, so I ran to the house. The man heard me and made to head me off before I could make it to the door.

He produced a short blade from his sleeve, and I was certain that he would stab me if I didn't beat him to the door. I was fumbling at the handle when he was on me. He brought the blade to my side, but there was a sound like clanging metal and the thief was blown clear off the porch. I looked down and saw that the blade was shattered on the ground next to me.

The thief got up and ran. I went quickly into the house and told Mother about the thief, and what had happened.

Mother checked my side, my arm, my leg, but there wasn't a scratch on me. I don't understand what happened. It's as if I was wearing an impenetrable armor, but really I was just wearing my work shirt and an old pair of Father's work pants. Mother couldn't explain what happened either. She told me to return to Father like I was supposed to and tell him about the thief. But she told me not to mention the attack and the broken blade. It was a strange story, she said.

Alexa sat for a long time, thinking about this entry until it started to make sense. Her mother had been in serious danger and was afraid for her life, when a strange power seemed to protect her. It was exactly the same as what had happened to Alexa with the enormous stranger she'd met in the wheat fields.

Maybe this was the power that Violet had been talking about. Michael's power manifested itself when he was angry, but maybe Alexa's power showed itself when she was afraid, like her mother.

But something was bothering Alexa. "How come this power didn't save her from the robbers?"

John shook his head wearily. "I don't know."

CHAPTER 7
COMINGS AND GOINGS

Alexa wanted to go after Michael as soon as he left, but John insisted that he would return after he cooled off. It took until the next morning, but John was right.

Michael walked in while John and Alexa were eating breakfast in the kitchen, which still smelled like burnt cedar, and casually sat down at the table. Neither John nor Alexa acknowledged him. He sat there, staring between them for a few seconds.

"Hello?" he said.

"Cooled off, Sorcerer?" John said through a mouthful.

"Yes." Michael turned toward Alexa. It was obvious he was still as angry with her as she was with him.

"You two apologize to each other," John said, standing up. He stood over them and folded his arms.

Alexa and Michael stared hard at each other, but neither said anything.

"I can wait here all day," John said.

Alexa looked away first. "I'm sorry," she muttered.

Michael got up from the table. "I'm sorry, too." Then he

93

turned toward his father. "Can I help you rebuild that side of the house?"

"Yes. That would be very helpful," John said. "Alexa and I have to go out to the farm to work, but you should probably clear the old timbers out wherever you can, and when I come home, we'll try to replace a few of them."

Michael nodded. "I'm sorry, Dad."

"It's okay. I'm just glad neither of you was hurt." John looked from Michael to Alexa. "Ready?"

Alexa nodded and got up. "I'll just be a few minutes. I don't want to leave this mess."

John nodded and walked out of the house. Alexa got up and started clearing up the plates and bringing them over to the washbasin. "I don't have time to make you anything, but there's bread —"

Michael grabbed Alexa's shoulders and turned her toward him. He brought his face close to hers. "What did you tell him?"

Alexa was shocked into silence for a moment, and then pulled herself free from Michael's grasp. She looked at him defiantly. "I told him everything."

"Did you tell him about Violet?" Michael asked.

"Of course. That old witch has been the cause of all this trouble," she said.

Michael leaned over her. "You don't know what you're talking about, Alexa. You just don't like Violet because she recognizes the power in me, and she knows I'm better than you. You just don't like being the loser of the family."

Alexa glared at him. "Why did you come back?" she said.

Michael didn't answer. He stomped away and went out the front door while Alexa finished washing the dishes. Once she was done, she walked out and started up the path toward the farm. She glanced around quickly for Michael, but he was nowhere to be found. Alexa doubted that he would clear the timbers like their father had asked. He was probably running back to Violet right now to tell on her.

As Alexa trudged through the barnyard that morning, she put Michael out of her mind and began tending the animals. She expected her father to be around, but she didn't see him.

When old Cal Verner walked by, Alexa asked him if he'd seen John, and Cal told her that Mr. Eckerly had sent him to the fields with the other men. Alexa knew that Mr. Eckerly was angry with her father, and that putting him on the regular crew of laborers was a sort of punishment.

In the middle of the morning, Duster and Mr. Eckerly came walking up the path from the fields. Mr. Eckerly was talking, and Duster was taking notes in a book as they walked.

Duster stopped just at the barnyard near Alexa and asked, "Is that everything?"

"Yes," Mr. Eckerly called over his shoulder, and went into the barn.

"Good morning, Alexa," Duster said.

"Hi, Duster," she said, scooping chicken feed out of a barrel with a pail.

He stepped forward. "Do you need help?"

"No," she said.

"I saw your father today in the fields. He looks good."

"Yeah. I think the fire yesterday really kind of woke him up," she said.

"I hope so," Duster said.

"Me, too. So, what are you taking notes for?" Alexa asked.

"Oh, I have to go to Coyne Village and buy some supplies at the market," he said.

"Oh," Alexa said. That was the sort of job that Mr. Eckerly used to trust to her father.

Alexa had turned away from him, pretending to dig more feed out of the pail. She listened and could tell that he had not moved. It became apparent that he was waiting to continue their conversation.

When she turned, he was still staring at her. "That's good," she said, and made to walk off.

Duster rushed forward and put his hand out to stop her from leaving, but he didn't touch her. "Are you almost done? I have to take the wagon straight past your house. I can give you a ride back," he said.

Alexa was about to roll her eyes; it was not even a mile to her house — she certainly didn't need a ride. But as she looked at Duster's eager face, she could tell that he just wanted a chance to talk. Alexa decided that he probably deserved that much. He'd been there when her mother had died, and he had let her cry in his arms after the fire.

"Sure. Let me finish up, and I'll meet you back here in ten minutes," she said. She couldn't help noticing that Duster's eyes lit up when she agreed.

A few minutes later they clumped slowly along the path, Duster absentmindedly holding the reins of the chestnut mare pulling the wagon. They sat in silence for a few minutes, both looking at the path ahead.

Duster finally turned to her. "How do you like working on the farm again?"

"It's fine," Alexa said. "I like working with the animals. Well, everything except the pigs. Whenever I get close enough to put food in the trough, they get all excited, or scared, or whatever, and they start scrambling around the pen, banging into the fence. Today, when I was balanced on the gate pouring food into the trough, one of them hit it and I almost fell in. I wouldn't want Mr. Eckerly to see that."

96

Duster laughed. "No. I guess not."

"I also feel a little guilty that I took Dad's job," she said. "I don't like the idea of him out in the fields under the blazing sun all day. That's hard work for him. I liked it better when he worked in the barn. It was easier for him. Safer."

"I know what you mean. Don't get me wrong—I'm glad that Mr. Eckerly trusts me enough to send me on errands like this. But I know that this is something he used to ask your father to do."

"I just hope that Dad keeps it together," she said, frowning.

"Why? You don't think your dad can control his drinking?"

"I hope so," Alexa said quickly. "He's all I have."

"You have Michael, too," Duster said. When Alexa didn't respond, Duster looked at her. "What's up? Is Michael leaving like you thought?"

Alexa shook her head.

At this point, they turned around the bend that brought the Flynn house into view. Duster pulled on the reins and the wagon came to an abrupt stop. Alexa looked over and saw Duster staring straight ahead with his mouth open.

Alexa turned and saw Michael standing near the back corner of the house as a burned timber rose slowly in the air. Michael moved his hands, and the timber floated slowly above the ground until it was above a whole pile of burned timbers. Then Michael dropped his hands and the timber crashed on to the pile.

"Did I just see that?" Duster said.

At the sound of his voice, Michael whipped around and brought his hands together, and pushed them up as if he was raising a sword. Duster rose from his seat on the wagon and floated into the air.

Alexa jumped down from the wagon and screamed.

"Don't hurt him!" She ran forward toward Michael, but she kept looking back at Duster over her shoulder. "Put him down! Gently!"

"Why?" Michael said. His eyes blazed as Duster rose to almost twenty feet in the air. Then Michael clenched his hands into fists and Duster screamed.

Alexa looked back. Duster was still in the air, but his face was tense with pain.

"What are you doing to him?"

"Squeezing." Michael's face was contorted with gleeful malice. When Alexa finally reached Michael she stopped in front of him. She'd thought of knocking him down, but if he lost his concentration she thought Duster might fall.

"Michael, listen to me," Alexa said. She slowly reached out her hand and put it on Michael's shoulder. "Put him down."

"He's going to run off and tell the others. Violet told me to protect the secret, and now you've told Father, and then you brought him here. I should kill him."

"Are you listening to yourself? He didn't do anything to you." Alexa straightened up. "I promise you he won't tell anybody," she said.

Michael opened his hands a little. "Well, little man. Are you going to run back and tell on me?" he said.

Duster hung in the air, but the force crushing him seemed to ease a little. He looked seriously from Alexa to Michael. He said, "No. I won't tell anyone, Michael. I swear."

"Fine." Michael turned away and put his arms down. Duster fell.

Alexa screamed, "No!"

Duster landed in the back of the wagon, which was thankfully full of straw. After a few seconds, he stood up, a look of confused relief on his face.

Alexa ran to him and scrambled onto the back of the wagon. She touched his face. "Are you all right?"

Duster gulped and nodded. "I think so." He patted himself warily, feeling for any pain.

Alexa jumped down and ran at Michael. He had his back turned and didn't turn around until she was almost on him. Alexa barreled into him with all her weight, and they went sprawling into the grass. She fell off him and pushed herself back to her hands and knees and leapt on him again. She punched ferociously at him.

Michael tried to bring one of his hands up toward her, but she punched it out of the way and kept pummeling him. Alexa's attack was so ferocious that Michael was too shocked to use his magic. Finally, Duster reached them and put his arms around Alexa's waist and lifted her into the air. He pulled her away as she continued to try to get at Michael.

Once Alexa was off him, Michael rolled to his side and coughed heavily. There was blood running from his nose, and his left cheek had a deep cut.

"Put me down!" Alexa screamed as she tried to get at Michael again. But Duster held fast, and when she finally lunged forward and got her feet to the ground, he yanked her back up again.

"Calm down," Duster whispered in her ear.

"I...will...not...calm...down!" Alexa hissed through gritted teeth as she continued to struggle.

Duster struggled to keep her feet off the ground. "Alexa, please. It's over."

Finally, Alexa stopped struggling and Duster put her down, but he didn't release her right away.

By this time, Michael had sat up and was eyeing them as he pinched his nose to try and stop the bleeding.

Duster shifted around Alexa before he let her go, and then walked to Michael. "Are you okay?" he said, holding out his hand.

Michael looked at Duster's hand and laughed. He got to his feet with a grunt. "I don't need your help. I suppose now you're going to run off and tell the whole farm about me," Michael said icily.

"No. I told you I wouldn't." Duster put his hands on his hips. "What was that, anyway?"

Michael laughed again and turned away. He began to walk quickly away into the woods.

Alexa had come to stand next to Duster. "Magic," she said quietly. Duster turned to look at her in disbelief. Alexa nodded. "I know. I didn't believe it either," she said. "But you can't tell anyone, Duster."

"I won't, but—" He stopped, apparently searching for the right words. "How?" was all he said as he turned back to watch Michael's retreating figure disappear into the trees.

"I don't know." Alexa hesitated for a moment, and then she plunged on nervously. "I can do it, too," she said.

Duster suddenly looked down at her. "You can do that?" He pointed at the pile of blackened timbers.

"No. I'm not as strong as Michael. I don't know how to control it, either," she said.

"So how does he know?" Duster's eyes were still wide and frightened.

"He has a teacher," she said.

"Oh," was all Duster said. Then suddenly, his eyes lit with recognition. "The fire—"

Alexa nodded. "Yeah. He started it."

"Alexa, he's dangerous," Duster said, his face tightening.

"Yeah. I know he is."

100

"So what are we going to do?" he said.

"Nothing. We're not going to do anything. We've just got to stay out of Michael's way, and hope he stays out of ours."

"What if he tries to hurt you?"

"Don't worry. I can handle Michael," she said. She tried to smile confidently. She wasn't sure she pulled it off, but Duster didn't say anything. "Are you sure you're okay from that fall?" Alexa said.

"Yeah. I am," he said, still frowning. "I guess I should probably get going if I'm going to get back before nightfall."

Alexa nodded.

"Are you sure—?" he began.

"Duster, don't worry. It'll be fine," she said. Then Alexa pushed herself up on her tiptoes and kissed Duster gently on the cheek.

Duster stood for a moment, stunned, then reached up and touched the spot where she'd kissed him. The corners of his mouth quirked a little, as if he was trying to suppress a smile.

"Okay, then," he said, turning back toward the cart. "I'll see you tomorrow." He was still sort of dazed as he walked away.

Alexa stood watching him climb back into the cart. "Be careful," she called.

"You too," he said, with a meaningful look toward the forest.

They stared at each other for a moment until Duster finally gathered up the reins and urged the horse forward.

But Alexa didn't have to wait until the next day to see Duster.

At dinner that night, Michael, Alexa, and John ate in silence. Michael and Alexa looked down at their plates, while John kept glancing between them. He was tired, but John ate ferociously. And he couldn't help smiling back when Alexa had smiled brightly at him after he'd asked for the biggest cup of water she could find to accompany his dinner.

John turned to Alexa first. "How were the animals today?"

Alexa nodded without looking up. "Good. I think one of the goats might be sick, though," she said.

He turned to his son. "Thanks for clearing those timbers," he said. Michael looked up and John saw him look at Alexa.

John glanced between them once more, and was just about to demand they both tell him what was the matter when there came frantic banging on the door.

Alexa heard Duster's voice from the other side of the door. "Mr. Flynn! Mr. Flynn, are you in there?"

Alexa made to get up and unlock the door, but John put his hand on her arm. He went to the door and opened it. Duster came rushing inside, breathless.

"Mr. Flynn, I found them," Duster said.

Alexa noticed that Duster looked sun-beaten and tired, and that his clothes were splattered with dirt. Duster's hands shook as he waited for John to respond.

"You found who, Duster?" John said.

"The men who killed Mrs. Flynn," he said.

John dropped his arms to his sides and Michael stood up from the table.

"Where are they?" Michael said.

"Just outside Coyne Village," he said, still looking at John.

"How did you find them?" John asked.

"It was luck, sir. I swear, just plain luck."

"Sit down and tell us about it, Duster," John said, indicating his empty chair at the table. Duster walked quickly around the table and sat down. His eyes had not left John's face.

"I was in Coyne market, and I had to go to the inn because Mr. Eckerly wanted some special barley for his wheat beer."

John nodded. He'd picked up the barley for Mr. Eckerly's beer many times from Otis, the innkeeper, whose ale was renowned for miles around.

"I was in there, and there were these two monks at the bar, but they didn't look like monks. They were really dirty. And they were blind drunk. All of a sudden one of them starts saying to the other, 'Can't you see I've still got the marks on my neck?' Well, I didn't think much of it, but the other one says, 'We were lucky to get away from that one, especially after stabbing those kids' mother.' They didn't say any more about it for a while, so I just stayed there listening for an hour or two, and when they left, I followed them. They staggered out of the village toward the woods, and I stayed far enough out of sight so that they wouldn't see me. Not that it mattered. They were so drunk I could've walked right behind them and they wouldn't have noticed me, but I followed them about a quarter of a mile outside the city to a small camp of tents. Sure enough, they met up with a third man. He was older and they kept calling him boss. But those were the men, Mr. Flynn. I know it was them. And I know where their camp is."

John had been nodding along as Duster talked, but even after he finished, he didn't say anything for a long time.

"What are you going to do, Dad?" Alexa finally asked.

John hesitated and then said slowly. "Tomorrow, Duster and I are going to ride out there and find these men. Then we're going to bring 'em to Mr. Eckerly."

"I want to come, too," Michael said, eagerly.

"Yeah. I reckon we might need your help, Michael," John said.

"I'm coming too, then," Alexa said, standing up.

"No, you're not," John said.

"Do you expect me to wait here while everyone I care about

goes off to hunt those...those...." Alexa couldn't decide what word to use. "Men?"

John walked forward and wrapped his arms around her. "I'm sorry, Alexa. You can't come."

Michael glared at her triumphantly and stalked out the door. Meanwhile, Duster was looking down, refusing to meet her eyes.

"Dad?" she pleaded.

He pulled back slowly and shook his head.

CHAPTER 8
FIGHT AND FLIGHT

Alexa hardly slept that night. It was still dark when she decided to get out of bed. She walked slowly and quietly through the house. Michael was nowhere to be found. Alexa figured he was probably still with Violet, practicing his magic.

As she approached the door to John's room, she heard his heavy snoring. She watched him in the moonlight, his body rising and falling hypnotically. His face was relaxed. The soft lines on his forehead were barely visible as he lay with one arm hanging over the side of the bed. She closed the door quietly and stepped into the kitchen.

She lit a candle and began packing up food items into a sack so that John, Duster, and Michael had food for their journey. She packed two whole loaves of bread just in case. If the killers tried to escape, John, Michael, and Duster might have to follow them, and they'd need even more food than they would normally bring on a short trip like the one into Coyne Village.

Alexa also pulled out a small bag from under her bed and filled it with a few bread ends and some berries. She also cut a small chunk of cheese and wrapped it in oiled leaves before

105

putting it into the bag. She then put her bag back under her bed. Alexa dressed slowly in the dark, and put on a pair of work pants and one of her mother's work shirts. Then she also pulled out a pair of her mother's boots and put them on.

As she went back out into the kitchen, she looked out the window above the basin and saw a sliver of sunlight emerge. It created a line of deepest red upon the horizon. Alexa couldn't help but notice that it looked like a bloody wound separated the land and sky.

She turned to go awaken her father, but saw that his door was already open. John was sitting on the edge of the bed. He was already dressed, but was still rubbing the sleep from his eyes.

"Morning, Dad," Alexa said.

"Morning," he said.

"I'll make breakfast," she said.

A few minutes later, while John and Alexa ate in silence, the door opened and Michael came in. He bounced toward the table and picked up a slice of bread and stuffed it into his mouth. There were dark circles around his eyes, but he stood, chewing noisily, bouncing up and down on the balls of his feet. Michael looked back and forth between John and Alexa, but didn't say anything.

Just then, they heard a soft knock on the door. Michael opened it and Duster came in. He had a bow slung over his shoulder, as well as a quiver of arrows.

Michael touched the bow. "Cool. Where'd you get that?"

Duster smiled. "It was my father's. Mother gave it to me when I was eight. I used to be able to hunt fairly well with it, but I haven't practiced in a long time. Years probably." He looked around the room hesitantly. "I just thought we might need it today."

106

"Maybe," John said, rising from the table. "Do you want anything to eat?"

"No thank you, sir," Duster said, standing at attention.

John came around the table and stood before Duster. "Michael," he said.

Michael came around and John reached out and put a hand on each of their shoulders. "Today could be very dangerous," he said. "Those men will not want to be taken. They're either going to run or they're going to fight like their lives depend on it—because they do. But we're going to stop them and bring them in. Mr. Eckerly will decide their fate. I don't want any killing if we can help it, but be ready to defend yourselves."

"You don't want to kill those animals that killed Mom?" Michael spat.

John looked at him thoughtfully for a moment before he spoke. "A couple of days ago, I'd have said there was nothing I'd like more than to kill those men. But someone," John turned his head slightly to look over at Alexa, "made me realize that the only way to remember your mother, to really honor her, is to keep living the best we can. To live honestly…and to take care of each other."

Alexa felt a single tear on her cheek. She looked past her father and saw Duster smile at her. She wiped the tear quickly and gave him a weak smile before she looked down.

"Let's go," Michael said, picking up the bag of food that Alexa had packed and walking out the door. John picked up his axe and unwrapped it. He also took the largest kitchen knife and put it into his belt. He stared after Michael for a moment and sighed, but followed.

"I won't let anything happen to them, I promise," Duster said.

Alexa looked up at his determined face. "You can't promise

that, Duster. You don't know what's going to happen."

He nodded. "I'll do my best."

"I know you will," she said, turning away.

"See you later," she heard Duster call as he headed out the door.

After they walked out, she closed the door behind them and listened. Alexa could hear John giving them instructions. She pressed her ear against the door until their voices faded away. Then she ran into her room and yanked the small bag of food she had packed for herself out from under the bed.

Alexa hoisted the bag over her shoulder, then went into the kitchen and picked up a knife. She started to put it in her belt then stopped. Alexa laid it back down on the table. She turned decisively and headed out the door.

Alexa walked slowly in the brush off the edge of the trail, stopping every so often to listen for the sounds of Michael, Duster, and her father ahead. She didn't want them to catch her following them.

She was also glad to be off the trail and in the shade. Alexa knew where Coyne Village was, so she didn't need to catch up with them until they reached it. Then, she would have to get close enough to follow without being seen, because she didn't know exactly where the camp was.

At one point, she stopped around the bend before a straightaway. She peeked slowly around the brush and saw the three of them in the distance. John's broad shape walked between Duster and Michael.

Alexa figured that they were about a quarter mile ahead of her, which was a good distance. She could stay hidden, and yet she could make up that ground easily when they reached the village. Alexa walked slowly and carefully, only stopping once to drink water from a small creek. She also ate the small lump of cheese, knowing it wouldn't make it far in the heat. Alexa still had the berries and the bread for rest of the day.

About noon, Coyne Village rose out of the valley before her. She could still make out the shapes of her father, brother, and Duster nearing the small cluster of buildings.

She continued to walk slowly until they disappeared from view, and then she began to jog toward the squat buildings that surrounded the small marketplace in the center. When she came to the edge, she stopped and looked around. Alexa saw Duster leading John and Michael into an inn across the square, and she knew that he was showing them where he'd found the men the day before. She waited, peeking out from behind the building every few seconds. After about five minutes, Alexa saw Duster lead them out the door, headed out of the village on the other side. She quickly began to walk through the square to catch up to them.

She bounded around a cart full of draperies and broke into a run as she saw them turning down a dark path into the woodlands on the far side of the town. An old man yelled, "Hey!" as she kicked up dirt near a small stand of pewter bowls and spoons. Alexa didn't turn to look at him.

Once she reached the path, Alexa stopped and listened. She thought she could faintly hear footsteps ahead of her. She walked slowly and cautiously, trying not to make any noise. She continued slowly, peering around bushes and holding her breath and listening every time she thought she heard the sound of footsteps or voices near. After about a quarter of a mile, Alexa heard the sound of many voices rising, and she realized that they were near the small encampment that Duster had described.

She stopped and found a small elm with a narrow trunk, and climbed it. From there, Alexa lay along a branch and strained to look ahead through the trees.

After a moment of her eyes adjusting, she saw it—a small encampment of about six tents. There was a small ring of stones in front of a couple of the tents. There were blackened timbers in it, but there was no fire.

A woman stood, holding a small child tightly against her chest while the child cried softly. She was making whooshing noises as she bounced up and down.

Alexa looked past the woman and saw a face she recognized. The swarthy-faced robber who Michael had burned was sitting in front of one of the tents. He seemed to be nodding off. There was a short knife clutched tightly in his hand.

Suddenly, Alexa heard her father's voice and saw him emerge from the trees to approach the robber. John's hands were empty. She couldn't see Michael or Duster.

"Hello, friend," John said. The swarthy-faced man sat up, fully alert. Alexa saw him slide the knife under his leg, out of sight. She hoped that her father had seen it before he hid it.

The robber made no response, but watched John warily as he approached. John stopped about ten feet in front of him and stood with his arms folded. He stood in silence for what seemed an eternity until the robber finally spoke. "What do you want?" he said.

"I want to know if you've ever been on Mr. Eckerly's farm," John said.

"Eckerly? Never heard of him. Don't get around much. Usually just stay around here." The robber's eyes were scanning around him as he spoke to Alexa's father.

"Is that so?" John said. "What if I told you that some of the men on this farm said they saw you robbing houses on Mr. Eckerly's land? That you even killed a woman?"

"Dunno what you're talking about," the swarthy-faced

man said, moving his hand onto his lap. Alexa was sure he had the knife in his palm.

Suddenly, Alexa felt rather than saw movement from directly below her. An old man in a grey tunic stumped slowly and quietly through the trees. He held a long knife in his hand. The old man stopped and was staring at John's back.

Alexa couldn't tell if the swarthy-faced robber had noticed his boss standing in the trees. If he did, he made no sign of it.

"Well, guess what? We're going to take you and a couple of your friends to this Mr. Eckerly and find out if you're telling the truth. If you are, he'll let you go, no hard feelings. But I've got a feeling that when we get back to the Eckerly farm, there's gonna be some trouble," John said.

"There ain't gonna be no trouble, because I ain't going nowhere," the robber said.

Suddenly, several things happened at once. The swarthy-faced robber jumped to his feet and lunged at John. The knife gleamed in a stream of sunlight that penetrated the trees.

The old man below her ran out at John, faster than Alexa could've imagined. The old man had almost reached her father when Duster appeared out of nowhere and blindsided him. Duster and the old man tumbled to the ground and began fighting. Duster quickly gained the upper hand and pinned him to the ground. He punched the old man in the face and dug his knees down into his shoulders to keep him where he was.

John had sidestepped the swarthy-faced robber, and produced the kitchen knife that he had stuck in the back of his belt. The two men circled each other. John was almost a foot taller and broader than the robber.

Michael was nowhere to be found, but suddenly, the small pudgy robber who had killed their mother sprang out of from one of the tents and barreled into John from the side. Alexa's

111

father hadn't been ready for it. John hit the ground and rolled quickly to his feet while the swarthy-faced man lunged at him again. The pudgy robber had fallen hard after trying to tackle John, but was scrambling to his feet.

Alexa swung herself to the underside of the branch and let her feet drop before letting go and racing forward toward the tents.

"Hal!" The swarthy-faced robber yelled to the pudgy man to alert him that Alexa was coming up behind him, but it wasn't in time. Alexa reached him before he could turn and leapt onto his back, locking her arms around his neck. He straightened up and tried to shake her off, but she brought her heel down hard into the back of the robber's knee and he fell forward.

He suddenly brought his elbow up into her nose and she let go. Alexa kicked him in the back before he could turn and attack her. The pudgy robber sprawled forward into the dirt.

Alexa saw the face of a greasy child peeking out of one of the tents. The woman holding the baby was huddled near the entrance of her tent, watching the fray.

Suddenly, out of the corner of her eye, Alexa saw Michael emerge from the trees on the other side. He raised his arms and all three of the robbers were launched into the air and hung there, staring around incredulously.

John was bent double, blood dripping from his mouth and breathing hard. Duster had just pushed himself to his feet and stared up at the robbers, who hung in the air like leaves on the wind.

Alexa was panting and wiping the blood from her nose with her sleeve.

"Put them down, Michael," John said between breaths.

Michael's didn't seem to notice his father. He spoke in a low dangerous voice to the men floating above him. "Do you remember me?"

Michael opened his hands further and the robbers flew higher. The old man rose through some branches and tried to grab on, but couldn't. The pudgy robber started to scream. "Help! Help!"

Michael twisted his fingers and the pudgy man's voice suddenly died away. Alexa could see that he was still trying to scream, but no sound was coming out.

John had come forward to stand next to Michael. John stared up at the robbers and then looked at his son. "It's over. Put them down."

Alexa looked into Michael's face and saw fury as he turned to each robber. Michael whispered something that Alexa couldn't hear.

"What's happened to them?" Duster's voice was loud and unnatural in the small forest encampment.

Alexa looked up and saw that all three of them had gone limp. Each of their heads hung to the side.

Suddenly, Michael lowered his hands and the bodies crashed to the ground.

Duster ran forward to the body closest to him, the old man, and flipped him on to his back. He put his head down on the old robber's chest. Duster's eyes stared at Michael with terror as he whispered, "He's dead."

"They're all dead," Michael said. "They were dead before they hit the ground." There was a strained, hysterical look on Michael's face.

Michael spread his arms wide and swept them in an arc before himself, and suddenly the tents all burst into flames. Alexa heard the woman with the baby scream, and suddenly several people, mostly women and children, burst out of the tents.

One young girl with filthy, matted hair ran in a circle, screaming because her dress was on fire. Duster ran up and grabbed her by the arms to stop her moving, and stepped on the flames until they went out.

Suddenly, Michael fell forward onto his knees. John grabbed Michael's shoulder to keep him from falling on his face. John stared at Michael as he held him up. Michael was breathing hard, his eyes glassy and unfocused.

Alexa ran up and knelt in front of him. "What's the matter?" she said.

But Michael couldn't answer—he was unconscious. John and Alexa lowered him to the ground.

"Stay with him," John ordered, and got up and ran to the nearest tent. He poked his head in and back out again. "Nobody in here. Duster, help me! See if there are people in these tents. Get them out!"

Duster ran over to the farthest tent on the other side and looked in. The two of them ran to each tent and looked for people. They found a few. One old woman looked as if she'd been sleeping when they dragged her out and sat her gingerly against a tree. Then they went around and tried to put out the flames, but it was a slow, difficult process, as it was dry and there wasn't any water around.

Eventually they extinguished the fires. The people who lived in the camp sat huddled together, watching John and Duster. Every once in a while, their eyes would flit over to where Michael was lying in front of Alexa, slowly reviving.

The sweltering afternoon, combined with the residual heat from the flames, was nearly unbearable. Alexa felt that she would almost pass out herself as she spoke quietly to Michael, rubbing and lightly slapping his cheeks to rouse him.

After a few minutes, Michael opened his eyes and pushed

114

himself up to his elbows. He breathed heavily but did not speak.

Suddenly, John stood above them. "Let's go. Now," he said.

Alexa got to her feet. Duster and John pulled Michael up and half carried him out of the clearing back toward the path.

Once they were away from the clearing, Alexa was happy to feel a soft breeze. It was much cooler once they reached the path that wound through the woods toward Coyne Village.

Alexa looked over her shoulder and John and Duster were still on either side of Michael, but not holding him up any more. Michael was walking slowly, but under his own power. Alexa looked into Michael's face, but it was blank, as if he was sleepwalking with his eyes open.

They walked back up the path, and when they reached the clearing that lead to Coyne Village, John said, "Let's go around." So they skirted the clearing through the trees and went all the way around the small village. They moved quickly, hoping no one would see them in the shadows. Once they made it to the other side, they picked up the path again, walking more quickly.

John finally came forward to walk beside Alexa. His shoulders slumped as he walked wearily. "I told you not to come," he said.

Alexa looked up at him. "I know," she said. She held his gaze for a moment and then looked forward. "I couldn't do it," she continued. "I couldn't wait around to find out if you all died."

John put his arm around her. "I know," he said.

"What are we going to do, Dad?"

John turned around to look back at Michael, who was still walking dazedly next to Duster. "I don't know. This is serious."

Alexa nodded.

It was nightfall when they finally reached the house. John

leaned his axe on the wall next to the door. Michael went right to the table and sat in a chair. He hadn't spoken the entire way home.

Duster stood uncomfortably in the doorway until Alexa pulled him inside by the arm. "C'mon. I'll make dinner," she said.

John turned to them. "Sit," he said.

The three of them watched as John went to the basin and rinsed his hands. He spread some water through his brown hair. John then pulled open the bag of food he'd been carrying and dumped the contents on the table between Michael, Alexa, and Duster. "Eat," he said.

Alexa didn't realize how hungry she was until she grabbed the small loaf of bread before her. She tore it in half and bit into it. She offered the other half to Duster, who took it, but didn't eat it.

Instead, Duster looked at John. "What are we going to do?" he asked.

At this point, John sat down at the table and looked at his son. "Michael. What happened back there? You killed them."

Michael seemed to finally awaken from his reverie. "Of course I killed them," he said.

"But Michael —"

"But what? Those animals killed my mother! Your wife!" He yelled. "We were going to *bring them in*," Michael whined sarcastically. "You are weaker than I ever imagined, Father."

"What about the tents?" Alexa broke in.

"What about them?" Michael didn't even look at her. He was still staring at his father.

"You could've killed innocent women and children," Alexa said.

Michael got to his feet and his voice was high and hysterical.

116

"No one is innocent, Alexa!"

The entire house shook with Michael's words. John and Duster both looked at the creaking walls uncertainly. Alexa never took her eyes from her brother's face.

"You are mad!" she said.

And faster than she ever thought he could move, Michael slapped Alexa across the face. She felt the stinging in her cheek and fell to the floor. She could hear John and Duster's chairs scrape against the wood as they rose to grab him. As she turned back toward the table, she saw Michael had grabbed Duster by the arm, and she could hear his flesh burn beneath Michael's hands.

John was transfixed in horror as Duster crumpled into a heap onto the table, howling in pain.

Alexa screamed, "No!" and Michael was blown backward into the wall next to John's bedroom door. He was pinned as if by invisible chains—he couldn't move his arms, legs, or head off the wall.

Alexa stood up and walked toward him. Michael's face was strangely boyish as he stared at her in shock. "You're a monster," she said.

Alexa felt a burning hatred she had never felt before. She wanted to hurt Michael. She wanted him to feel the agony and fear he seemed to enjoy inflicting on other people. She didn't know how to do it, but if Alexa's power could hold Michael against the wall, Alexa felt she might strangle him with her bare hands. There was a split second in which Alexa wanted to feel that power—she wanted to see the life drain out of Michael's arrogant face. But suddenly she heard her father's voice, barely a whisper in their crowded cabin.

"Let him go," he said.

Suddenly, Alexa's anger left her. She breathed deeply and

gained control of herself. After she rubbed her eyes wearily, she was shocked to see that Michael was still pinned to the wall, his eyes darting back and forth in fear. Alexa's anger had left her, and she could think and action rationally, and yet Michael was pinned to the wall by her power. Alexa could feel the power coursing through her arms, legs, and chest.

"Michael," she said, "I'm going to release you. You have to remain calm. You have to listen to me. What you're doing—it isn't right. You're using your power and hurting others. You've become a danger to the farm. And to us." She looked down. "I don't want you to become a monster just because you have this power. You can control it. You can control yourself and be a good person, but you have to try."

Alexa took another breath and thought about releasing Michael, and it happened. He put his feet on the ground and shook his arms out as he walked forward.

His face was an inscrutable mask.

"I am...." He raised his palm toward her. "A danger to you."

A moment before he put his hand up, Alexa felt what Michael was about to do and flung her arms up over her face. There was a rushing sound, and a concussive blast blew all of them off their feet. The walls rattled ominously.

Alexa was sprawled on her back, but unharmed. She rolled to her side and saw John, blinking stupidly after being blown into the table. Duster was pushing himself up already, but Michael, who had been blown back into the wall again, shook off the blow and ran for the door. No one made a move to stop him.

They heard his heavy footsteps on the porch and the rustle of his boots on gravel, and then all the sounds were gone. Michael had run off into the night.

CHAPTER 9
BROKEN WORDS

When Alexa awoke the next morning, her entire body ached. She rose slowly and pulled on her clothes. She sat down on her bed and listened to the noises coming from the kitchen. Someone was milling about the basin, and she heard the clatter of bowls being set on the table.

She opened the door and was surprised to find John ladling soup into the two bowls on the table. Alexa noticed that there was no bowl in front of Michael's chair.

John turned to her as she yawned in the doorway. She put the back of her hand to her mouth, and saw when she removed it that there was blood on it. The cut on her lip from the robber's elbow had broken open and was bleeding again.

"Morning," John said. "You look like hell."

"I feel like it," Alexa said, and lumbered into the kitchen and fell into her chair.

"Maybe you shouldn't come into work today. I'll explain it to Mr. Eckerly and take care of the animals."

Alexa had to swallow the hot soup before she answered. "That's okay. I'll go to work. I only work in the morning."

"You sure?"

Alexa nodded. She looked across the table at Michael's empty seat, and suddenly felt sad. It was wonderful to have her father back to himself again, but now Michael was gone, and she didn't know how they were going to get him back.

John, seeing her stare across the table, spoke as if in answer to her thoughts. "After work tonight we're going to find that old witch and get him back."

Alexa nodded, but she couldn't meet John's eyes. She had a feeling that it was going to be very difficult to convince Michael to abandon his studies with Violet and come home.

A few minutes later, Alexa and her father were walking up the path toward the farm. John looked straight ahead as he spoke to his daughter. "Before I start today, I'm going to see Mr. Eckerly and tell him what happened."

Alexa looked up doubtfully. "What are you going to tell him?"

"Everything. He needs to know everything," John said. "He needs to know about the witch on his land and what Michael is capable of, and how those robbers are lying dead in the forest outside of Coyne. That there's a whole encampment of people who might not be too happy with us."

Alexa nodded. "He's going to be mad."

"Sure he will," John said. "He's got every right to be."

"What if he throws us off the land?" Alexa asked.

"He won't," John said. "Don't you worry."

John and Alexa separated as they reached the barn. Alexa went in to begin tending the animals, and John walked on to a large wagon where Mr. Eckerly was talking to a couple of the field hands.

"Good luck, Dad," she said.

John winked over his shoulder at her.

It wasn't until much later in the morning that Alexa saw her father again. He was coming back in with a wagon full of timber from one of the woodlands Mr. Eckerly owned just north of the farm. He looked serene as he whistled while the horse pulling the wagon continued its slow trot toward the farm.

Alexa had just emptied her feed pail, and dropped it on the ground. She looked quickly around and, not seeing Mr. Eckerly, ran up to her father.

"Almost done?" John said, squinting against the bright sunlight.

"Yes. What did he say, Dad?" Alexa said as she walked next to the horse.

"He was angry. Damn angry. He wants Michael and the witch off his land, and he's going to Coyne Village himself to see the encampment."

"What are we going to do?

"Like I said, tonight we're going to get Michael, and then we're going to run that witch off Mr. Eckerly's land," John said.

"It won't be that easy, Dad. She's powerful," Alexa said.

John looked down into the pale oval of her face and saw the fear in her eyes. "Don't worry. Between you, me, and Michael, she'll get the message and leave."

That night, John and Alexa left the house shortly after sundown. John locked the door while Alexa stood on the steps, looking up at him and twisting her hands nervously.

John walked slowly but confidently. Alexa had begged him to take his axe, but he'd refused and only had the large kitchen knife in his belt.

They walked slowly through the haze left behind by the recently vanished sun. There was a light breeze that fought its way through the summer heat. It blew the grass blades around their feet as they made their way into the woods.

The breeze died once they were within the trees, and it was even slower going in the heavy darkness. They had discussed bringing a torch, but decided against it, worried that it might attract attention.

The journey seemed to take forever, and Alexa jumped at the slightest sounds of the night, afraid that she might hear Violet's creaking laugh and suddenly feel the power of her magic rain down upon them.

When they finally came to the clearing, John walked out without hesitation. Alexa stopped at the edge of the trees and drew her breath before following her father.

Sure enough, the failing light showed them Violet's small cottage, and Michael and Violet standing in front of it. Michael was facing Violet, and she was speaking to him intently. She moved her hands in small circles, demonstrating what she wanted him to do. Neither of them made any indication that they had noticed John or Alexa.

John stopped in the center of the clearing and said, "Excuse me." His voice echoed loudly.

Michael turned around. He stood with his feet apart and folded his arms. Violet raised her head and peered at John.

Suddenly, Alexa heard Violet's creaking laughter, and watched her round shoulders slowly move up and down.

"I knew you would come," she hissed.

"I've come to get my son, and to tell you that Mr. Eckerly will not allow you on his land. You must leave," John said.

The old woman laughed again. "Of course, of course. But let us ask your son whether or not he will abandon his studies."

John's voice boomed in the night. "It's not a question." Then John looked at Michael. "Come here, son."

Michael didn't move. He glared at his father.

"It seems that the young man does not wish to come with

you." Alexa could hear the glee in Violet's voice. "He learns much from me. He gains in power every day. He is able to do things that people like you could only dream of."

"Like kill people?" John said.

Violet stood erect for the first time, and Alexa was surprised by the change. She was taller, and somehow seemed more powerful than Alexa had ever remembered seeing her. "Yes," she said. Her voice no longer creaked, but was full of breath and command. "He can hurt who he wants. He can kill his enemies. His power is great. You would not begrudge him his power."

"You're twisting him into some kind of monster!" John said. He took a few steps forward and pulled the knife out of his belt. "Listen, old one, you're leaving this land and my son is staying here. Now get your things and go."

Violet stared thoughtfully at John, and then she bent forward. She was suddenly the doddering old woman again. "Michael," she said, "this is your test. Destroy them."

Michael brought his hands down to his sides and turned toward Violet. "What?"

"Destroy them," she hissed. "You must prove your loyalty. If you are to truly realize your power, you must be free of the hold that your family has upon you. They will convince you that your power is less important than they are. Your power will fade. You will be nothing."

Michael turned back to face them just as John ran forward, brandishing the knife. Michael turned his face away as he raised his hands. He spoke a word softly and a flash emanated from his hands and hit John in the chest. John crumpled to the ground, a look of shock on his face as he fell.

"No!" Alexa ran forward and knelt next to her father. He lay on his back, breathing raggedly. His eyes darted around wildly. Alexa picked up his head gently and cradled it. "Dad.

Dad!" she whispered, but he was unable to answer her.

He was completely limp in her arms. His powerful arms were lifeless and heavy as she tried to lift him up.

Violet strode forward quickly, faster than either Michael or Alexa had ever seen her move. She stood above Alexa, looking down at them. "Good. Good," she said. She turned back to Michael. "He will be dead within minutes. It wasn't your best effort, but it'll be enough."

Michael still had his face turned away. He looked like a small child afraid to peer into the darkness of his closet.

"Kill her, too," Violet said.

"I can't," Michael said.

"You must," Violet said. "She would destroy me. She would destroy you as well. She is jealous of our power, Michael. She is not as talented as you. She is unwilling to make the commitment. That is why she hates us. Us—we who commit ourselves to the power of magic, who sacrifice so that we may call upon it to mold the world as we see fit. She's afraid of that power, just as your father is. She must be destroyed."

Alexa laid her father's head gently back onto the grass. His breathing had become even more shallow. She kissed his forehead. As she bent her head, she saw the glint of the kitchen knife just a few feet away. She glanced up and Violet was still standing there, with her back turned, facing Michael. She lunged for the knife and sprang up at Violet.

Just as she would have brought the knife into the old woman's back, she felt the force of Michael's power slam into her and quickly rose in the air. The knife dropped harmlessly to the ground.

She looked down at Michael and saw him close his fist tighter, and she felt the pressure as her arms pressed into her body. She couldn't breathe, and Alexa felt like her collarbone was about to snap. She realized that Michael was squeezing the life out of her.

Violet's creaking laugh was the only sound Alexa heard, until suddenly, she felt an intense rush of pain and nearly passed out. She suddenly felt Michael loosen his grip and she hung limply in the air, her head hanging to one side.

"I'm sorry, Alexa," she heard Michael whisper. Then she felt the rushing force of gravity take hold and hit the ground hard, but she was still alive.

Alexa felt like the air had been siphoned from her lungs and she couldn't move — not because she was hurt or dying, but because she could feel Michael's power holding her in place.

"You have done well, my young one," Violet said.

Violet raised her hand and a long, crackling bolt of electricity emanated from it. She brought her hand down and the lightning whip wrapped itself around Michael. The whip raised him high off the ground and turned him to face the witch.

"What are you doing?" Michael struggled, but the whip held him fast.

"You belong to me now," Violet laughed. "I had to push your power to its limits. I had to see for myself what you would be able and willing to do. Your power will be mine. I shall be reborn!" She turned to walk off into the woods with the whip carrying Michael behind her.

Alexa lay there for several minutes until, suddenly, the force that held her motionless broke. She got to her feet warily. Alexa realized that could mean only one of two things: Either her brother had willfully freed her from his spell, or else Michael was dead.

Alexa couldn't worry about that now. She ran back to where her father lay in the grass. His eyes were closed. Alexa leaned down and pressed her ear against his heart, and heard the faint heartbeat. She looked around wildly, not knowing what to do or where to go.

She jammed her hands beneath his body and tried to pull him up. "C'mon, Dad," Alexa muttered. His limp body was much too heavy for her.

Alexa stood back for a moment and thought about Michael and Violet. They were able to use their magic to move things without touching them. She screwed her face up in concentration and imagined her father rising in the air. But he didn't move. His eyes were still closed.

It was then that all hope left her. Alexa's head hung limply, and she felt the empty tears streaming down her face. She felt a burning in her throat and stomach as she bent down and put her hands on her knees. She could barely stand. There was nothing she could do.

Then from behind her, Alexa heard a voice.

"He will not die...yet," it said.

Alexa spun around and saw, standing just a few feet from her, the wild woman she had seen at the woodland council. The woman was tall, even taller than her father. The moonlight illuminated the woman's coarse tunic—it appeared to be of deepest green, and her bare arms stood out strikingly as her alabaster skin gleamed.

The woman's vivid red hair was the color of blood in the moonlight. As she stared at Alexa, her green eyes glittered brilliantly. The woman made no move nor said anything else. She seemed to be waiting for Alexa to reply.

Alexa pushed herself up and wiped her eyes hastily. "Who are you?" she said.

The woman's deep voice seemed to come not from her mouth, but from all around Alexa, as if it was carried to her by the night wind.

126

"I am Donan," she said.

"My father is dying," Alexa said.

"Yes. His light is almost out," Donan said.

"Can you help him? Please?" Alexa begged.

"No. I cannot. Death is a natural part of life. It is not for me to interfere."

Alexa felt her strength leaving her again. "But you don't understand," she said before she bent down and put her hands on her knees again. She felt like she might be sick.

When Alexa looked up, she saw other figures emerging from the darkness of the woods and coming toward her. They were the other members of the council she had seen sitting on the stumps in the grove.

Caelan, the warrior, stalked forward quickly. His rippling muscles gleamed with sweat against the light of the moon. His face, edged by the long scar, was eager with anticipation.

"He's mine!" The warrior boomed. "He was the loser in a battle. I'll take him now."

As the wheezy little man walked unsteadily forward, he coughed wetly into his fist before stopping a few feet behind Donan.

The tall, handsome man in cerulean robes came up and stood next to Donan. His face was lit with a sneering smile.

"Tut, tut, tut," he said. "The treachery of the young. It's Violet's special talent, isn't it?"

"Quiet, Breg," Donan said, still looking at Alexa.

Alexa looked around at each of them. Caelan looked as if he would rush forward at any moment—he was impatiently pawing the ground.

"Will you help me?" she cried, turning to each of them, one by one.

The little man with the cough refused to meet her eyes, but

began to wipe his mouth with a filthy rag. Breg's chest rose in a short silent laugh, but he made no response.

It was the woman who answered her again. "None of us can help you," she said. "But you can help yourself."

"What do you mean?" Alexa said. She was furious. These people were standing around, talking in riddles, and her father was lying unconscious, losing his life with every second they wasted.

It was then that one last shape emerged from the trees. Alexa recognized the small shape of the little girl who had sat at the head of the woodland council. Her skin shone in the night. She seemed to glow brighter than the moon as she approached quickly, and walking straight past Donan and Breg, she knelt down in front of John's body.

Alexa watched her reach down and pass her slender hand over John's eyes. His shallow, ragged breathing became slower, deeper. He looked as if he was in a restful sleep.

"He is alive," the little girl said. "He will remain alive...." She looked up at Alexa. "For as long as it takes you to find the crimson lady and destroy her." The little girl's face was serene. She spoke as if in a dream.

"What? Who?" Alexa blinked down at the stunning face.

The little girl put her hands out. Breg and Donan came forward and each took one and pulled her to her feet.

"You know her as Violet. She is an ancient witch of great power."

"Is she going to hurt Michael?"

"Yes. She means to take his magic and his life," the little girl said simply.

"I don't understand. How do I stop her? How do I save Michael? How do I save my father?" Alexa said.

"She is just a child. She is hardly worthy," Breg said

suddenly, fiercely.

"She has sought the burden, just as our queen said she would," Donan said. Neither of them were looking at Alexa — they were staring down at the figure of the little girl, who was still staring at Alexa with her brilliant eyes that seemed to shine with starlight.

After a moment's silence, the little girl spoke. Her voice was a melodic soprano, rising above the wind and the noises of the night.

"Alexa Flynn, we are the Council of Calamity." The little girl turned and spread her arm to indicate each of her companions. "We oversee all the ills of the world in order to maintain the natural order and balance. Each has his or her role to play. He...," she waved her arm toward the gigantic warrior, "is Caelan. He inspires anger and jealousy in the hearts of men to drive them to violence and war. This is Breg." She indicated the man in the cerulean robes. "He spreads falsehoods and betrayal through the world. This is Donan." She waved her arm at the woman this time. "She controls the awesome powers of the natural world. Storms, drought, and flood are signs of her despair. That," she indicated the wheezing little man, "is Hack. He spreads famine and disease silently through the land."

"And who are you?" Alexa asked the little girl.

"Don't interrupt the queen," Caelan bellowed.

The little girl smiled. "Few know my true name. For my name is the only power the world has against the destruction that Breg, Donan, Caelan, and Hack wield. I am known to most as the Queen of Calamity," she said. "We've come to offer you a bargain for the life of your father."

"Whatever it is, I will pay it," Alexa said at once.

"You cannot pay for it, you silly girl," Breg said.

The little girl raised her hand, and Breg, who had seemed

about to say more, fell back into moody silence.

"Breg is right. You cannot pay for it with gold or silver. What we offer is this: You are to destroy the crimson lady, the witch you know as Violet. In doing so, you may save the life of your brother. As a part of the bargain, I will allow John Flynn to slumber undisturbed until such time as you confront the witch. If you are able to destroy her, he will awaken and rejoin the world of the living. But if you fail, he shall pass into the shadow of death." The little girl took a shallow breath. "If you fail, you will likely join him," she added.

Alexa was angry. "You are all-powerful beings. Why don't you bring my father and brother back and go destroy Violet yourselves?"

"It's the burden of man to solve his own problems, not ours," Donan said.

Alexa looked to each of the calamities and found no reassurance in any of their faces. She looked down once more at the face of the little girl, who was studying her, a serious expression on her face. As Alexa looked at the queen, her eyes softened, and Alexa saw her own tears reflected in the shining face of the little girl.

Alexa drew her breath and stood as tall as she could. She said loudly and clearly into the night, "I accept your terms. What must I do?"

The queen came forward and took Alexa's hand. There was an ethereal lightness to the girl's touch. She led Alexa away from the others, walking toward Violet's small cabin.

As they walked hand in hand, the little girl spoke softly into the night air. "The one you know as Violet has upset the natural order of life for generations. She has lived many lifetimes by draining the life and magic of other sorcerers. She has been hiding for many years, unable to find a suitable prospect to prolong her life. We thought she would finally pass from the world this time, until she found you and your brother. The great danger arises from your brother's immense power. If she takes his power, her own will increase so that she will become nearly as great a force as any of the those you just met, except she will have no natural order to abide her. She will be able to create ruin and violence and death indiscriminately. She must be stopped."

It was at this point that Alexa's courage faltered once again. She slumped forward. "How am I going to stand against her? My power is so weak. I don't know any spells either."

The little girl looked up at her once more, her eyes shining starlight. "Spells alone will not overcome the crimson lady."

"Then what power will overcome her?"

The queen smiled. Alexa looked at the pale oval of her face and was dazzled by her radiance. "That is what you must discover," she said.

"Where do I begin?" Alexa asked.

The little girl pointed to Violet's small cabin. "Here," she said. "This is not the crimson lady's permanent home. She uses her power to conjure up dwellings when she travels, but you may find something that helps you within."

Alexa looked unsurely around the clearing. "What if she returns?"

"She will not return here. She has what she wants. She will bring your brother to her keep and prepare to take his power."

Alexa steeled herself and turned to go into the cabin, but just then she felt the light touch of the queen on her arm. When Alexa looked back at her, the little girl's face was creased with worry.

"You do not have long, Alexa," the queen said. "Her lair is not only well-hidden, but it is well-protected. The crimson lady has lived many lifetimes. She understands human weakness. She will try not only to kill you, but to take your humanity from you."

Alexa looked back to where the calamities stood around her father's body. "What about Dad?"

The queen said, "Donan will return him to your home. He will sleep until you confront the crimson lady. Then will his fate be decided."

Alexa nodded grimly and looked ahead into the dark cottage. She took a few slow steps forward and pushed heavily on the door. A creaking, not unlike Violet's laugh, sounded from the hinges. Alexa took a breath and plunged into the darkness.

She stumbled almost immediately on a chair and began to feel around cautiously, until her hand found a tabletop. She groped around until she found the candle on it, and continued to feel for matches, but there were none. Thinking of Michael's power, Alexa imagined a small flame in her hand and it sparked into existence. Instead of burning her, it felt like icy water running over her fingertips. She slowly brought her fingers to the wick and lit the candle.

She shook her hand until the flame disappeared from it, and picked up the candle. She walked slowly through the shadows of Violet's room, looking for anything that might help her find Violet's lair and save her brother.

Alexa opened every drawer in a small chest and found nothing but coarse clothing. She opened cabinets in the kitchen only to find bowls and small iron pots.

Alexa got down on her hands and knees and felt the floorboards, looking for a secret compartment or something, but found none. She walked slowly down the hall, her hand running along the wall, feeling for a secret door, and found herself in Violet's small bedroom.

There was a wooden bed, with a coarsely sewn mattress and blanket on it. Alexa looked around the room and saw only a small table next to the bed. There was an unlit candle on it. Alexa peered under the bed, but found nothing.

Alexa stood perplexed, staring around the sparsely furnished room. There were no pictures on the wall. There was no bookcase to examine.

Anger began to gnaw at Alexa's insides. She wanted to know where Violet was. She wanted to know what she was doing. She wanted the help of the council, but they were unwilling. She was never going to get anywhere and she knew it.

In a fit of frustration, she kicked out at the small table next to the bed. It toppled over onto its side, and Alexa could see a piece of parchment wedged into the drawer slot underneath it.

She knelt down and withdrew it. It was heavy, and as Alexa unfolded it, she recognized it as a plan of Mr. Eckerly's farm. She looked and saw that her own house was marked on the map—there was an oblong circle around it. That was no surprise. It appeared that Violet was simply marking the house of those she discovered who had the power.

She scanned the rest of the map, and was surprised to see a small X marked about six miles away in the woodlands to the northeast. There were no other marks on the map. Alexa folded it up and put it in her pocket. After one more cursory search through the house, she decided that there was nothing else to be found and walked back out the front door.

The horizon was edged with pink as Alexa came out into the clearing. She looked to the spot where her father lay a little while earlier to see that he, the queen, and the rest of the council of calamity were gone.

Alexa began the slow trek through the woods back home.

Fear whipped at her brain as she walked. What would she

find when she followed the map to the spot in the woods marked by the X? How would she find Violet's lair in time? Would she be able to save Michael? Would she be able to destroy Violet and save her father's life?

Alexa had no idea about any of it. She had no idea whether or not she would survive the dangerous journey she was about to undertake, but she thought about her father and her brother and decided that it didn't matter — she had to try.

CHAPTER 10
THE SURVIVOR'S TALE

When Alexa finally made it home, she found Duster asleep at her kitchen table, his face pressed against the wood. Duster's mouth hung open, and a small pool of drool had formed on the tabletop. Alexa stopped before him and wanted to reach out and touch his face, but she didn't.

She looked past him into her father's room and saw John was in the bed. Just as the queen had promised her, John slept peacefully, his chest rising and falling slowly, hypnotically.

Alexa knelt before the bed and passed her hand gently over her father's forehead. He didn't stir. Alexa hadn't really expected him to, but there was a small part of her that hoped he'd awaken. Alexa realized that whether or not her father ever opened his eyes again depended on her.

The thought did not console her. Alexa found a tide of panic rising in her chest and started to breathe raggedly, as if she'd been running hard. It was then that she felt Duster's hand on her shoulder. She turned and saw him yawn, trying to shake the sleep from his eyes.

"Are you okay?" he said.

Alexa nodded.

"What happened? I came here after work last night and knocked on the door. No one answered. I waited on the steps until nearly dawn. Then suddenly a tall woman walked out of the woods carrying your father. I yelled to her, and that's all I remember. I don't remember coming in here or putting your father to bed."

"You didn't. Donan did."

Duster's face wrinkled in confusion. "Who?"

Alexa told him all about the night before. She told him all about the confrontation with Violet, Michael's spells, and Violet taking her brother prisoner and vowing to steal his power. When she came to the appearance of the Council of Calamity, she went back and told him all about meeting the warrior, and following him into the grove and watching their meeting. Then she told Duster all about their appearance last night, and the bargain she'd made with the queen.

Duster stood with his mouth open for her entire explanation. Even after she finished, he continued to look dumbfounded, and said nothing for several minutes.

Alexa finally decided to leave Duster to his shock and began to move around the kitchen, finding any food she could and packing it into her small burlap bag.

Finally, Duster spoke. "What are you going to do?"

Alexa pulled out the map and held it out behind her. "I found this map in Violet's cottage, and I'm going to check out the X she put there."

Duster took the map and looked it over. Alexa turned around and watched him trace his finger from the farm up to where the X was marked. A grimace of confusion lingered on his face after he looked up.

"I'm coming with you," Duster said.

"No you're not."

"Yeah. I am," he said. "You're going to need me. I know the woods in that area better than anyone." He walked forward and took her hand. "I want to help."

Alexa pulled her hand away from his. "This is my fight, Duster."

"You don't have to fight alone."

As Alexa looked up at him, she saw concern and tenderness blazing in his blue eyes. He smiled weakly.

Alexa hugged him tightly. She didn't know what to say. Alexa couldn't get the words out, but she wanted to let Duster know how much his help would mean to her. She laid her head on his shoulder. He patted it gently.

"So you'll let me tag along?" he said.

Alexa laughed and pulled away from him. "Yeah. I guess," she said.

An hour later, Alexa and Duster were walking slowly through the forest, skirting the farm, hoping to avoid Mr. Eckerly or any of the other farm hands as they began their journey. Once they reached the river, they found a shallow place to cross. Even though Mr. Eckerly owned the land, it was still wild on this side. No one traveled through it unless they were hunting.

Alexa had left a letter to Mr. Eckerly on the kitchen table before they left, just in case he came to find out what was going on. It explained that John was very ill and not to disturb him, and that she, Michael, and Duster had gone off to find medicine for him.

They walked in silence for most of the journey. When they came to a marshy area around midday, Alexa found herself trudging into the mud. It was so deep it seeped into her boots.

There was a point near the end of the marsh in which Duster, walking a little ahead of her, came to solid ground again. He held out his hand and pulled Alexa onto a small outcropping of rock that led to a solid forest floor. As they continued to walk, Alexa looked down and saw that Duster was still holding her hand.

She didn't let go.

It was nearly sundown when they came within range of whatever was marked by the X on the map. Alexa wasn't sure what she was looking for.

"What do you think the X marks?" she asked. "A house? A cave? A grave, maybe?"

"I don't know. I think I've been through this area before, but I've never seen anything. Hopefully it's something that we'll notice. I'd hate to think that it's some small hidden sign and we just completely miss it," he said.

Alexa had been thinking along the same lines and sighed. "Me too," she said.

The sun had almost completely set before them when suddenly, as if emerging from the darkness, Alexa saw the ruins of a large stone house.

The house was enormous—larger even than Mr. Eckerly's manor house. There was a turret in the front that rose well above the line of the trees. A cobblestone walkway led up to a set of handsome oak front doors. One of the doors was hanging off its hinges.

The stonework was magnificent, with ornate carvings of angelic and demonic creatures in relief against flourishing columns and buttresses. The house was in disrepair, however. There were large cracks in the stonework, particularly on the west side, and heavy, damp moss grew out of them in many places. It looked as if the house had not been inhabited for a long time.

"This has to be it," Alexa said, her eyes still on the house.

When Alexa looked, Duster had walked off the cobblestone path to look at the side of the house. He was frowning at it. "I'm sure it is. But I've been through here before. I've never seen this place before. How is that possible?" he said.

Alexa shrugged. "I don't know." She walked up the cobblestones toward the doors.

"Wait. What if someone's in there? It could be a trap," Duster said.

Alexa had never thought of this. Could Violet have left the map behind hoping to lure Alexa off the farm to her death? She stopped, staring through the doorway into the dark hall. She couldn't make out anything.

"It might be, but we have to go in," she said.

Duster nodded. "Okay, let me go first." He started to rummage through his pack. Alexa knew he was looking for his flint to light a branch for light.

"I've got it," Alexa said. She stared into her hand and imagined the small flame emanating from her fingertips. Suddenly, the light was there. Alexa looked over at Duster and he was staring at the tiny flame.

"You do have magic," Duster said. He laughed in amazement and shook his head. "Okay, Sorceress. Lead the way," he said, and came to stand next to her.

Alexa reached out and grabbed Duster's hand with her free one. They walked forward and pushed open the oak door.

The hallway was large with a cracked marble floor. The walls were covered with heavy tapestries, each with large images of colorful birds set against mountain backgrounds. The hall led to a spiral staircase, wide enough for six or seven people to walk up, with a railing that Alexa could tell, even in the shadowy light of her flame, was a dull gold.

There were hallways on each side leading into the wings of the house, but Alexa stopped at the stairs, and with a little nod of her chin, motioned upward. Duster nodded and they slowly and quietly began to climb.

Alexa held her hand out before her as they walked. The tiny point of light emanating from her finger showed her rich carpet over highly polished wooden floors, and walls with brass sconces down the hallway that led to a series of rooms. The first was a sitting room, with chairs and a large golden harp sitting in the middle. There were spider webs visible between the strings. This room also had a large picture window, through which the moon now shone over an overgrown garden and a gazebo with a roof that had fallen in.

The next room was an opulent bedroom. A large, canopied bed dominated the room. Bookshelves built into the far wall sat across from a collapsed walnut desk missing two of its legs. Alexa couldn't help herself, and walked through this room to the bookshelves. She passed her finger up and down along the spines, reading the titles.

Duster remained in the doorway, peering into the darkness on either side of him as he waited for Alexa to return to his side.

Alexa had her back turned when she heard two short, heavy footsteps, a grunt, and then the sound of bodies coming together, and Duster's cry of pain as he was knocked to the floor.

Alexa ran back to the entrance and looked around, holding her finger before her. A few steps to her left, she saw Duster on the ground wrestling with a man in ragged clothing.

The light helped Duster locate his attacker, and he quickly brought an elbow down on the man's back. Alexa saw the body hit the floor. She expected the man to roll over quickly and jump to his feet, but he didn't. Meanwhile, Duster had jumped

140

up and was slowly backing away, looking at the man lying on the floor.

It was a shock when the man lifted his head and they saw the wrinkled face and gray stubble of an old man, wheezing with the effort from the fight. The man blinked stupidly up at the light emanating from Alexa's finger.

The man continued to breathe loudly, until he finally said, "You're too late."

"What?" Alexa and Duster said together.

"You're too late," the old man said, and finally rolled himself into a sitting position. "My master is already dead. She killed him. Him and the whole family."

"Who is your master?" Alexa said.

"Bartle Wilks. He was a sorcerer—like you, miss. That Violet came here pretending to offer him friendship, and then she attacked." The old man put his hand to his face and began to cry.

Alexa walked quickly around and began lighting the sconces in the hallway. Once there was enough light, she rubbed her fingers together and the small flame in her hand was extinguished.

She looked down at the old man. His wispy hair stood up around a large bald spot in the middle of his head. He was short, with a small belly from which sprung two thin legs. Alexa thought that when the old man stood up, those legs would barely support him.

The man sat with his hand over his face, crying for many minutes. Neither Duster nor Alexa moved. They just stared at each other. Alexa could feel her heart beating in her chest. She wanted desperately to know what happened here—what Violet had done—but she held herself in check. She waited patiently for the old man to gather himself.

When the old man finally started to control himself and he wiped his nose noisily on his sleeve, Alexa came forward and knelt near him.

"Who are you?" she asked.

"My name is Bothwell. I've been Mr. Wilks's servant for many years. His family was like my family. And now they're all dead." The old man looked as if he might start crying again, so Alexa reached out and touched his shoulder.

"Mr. Bothwell, when was Violet here?" Alexa said loudly, trying to keep him focused.

"Maybe a month, maybe two. I've lost track of the days since it happened," Bothwell said.

"A month? But this house looks like it's been abandoned for years," Duster said, looking around.

"Well, Mr. Wilks built it with magic, didn't he? So when he died, the house started to die, too, I guess. I don't know," Bothwell said.

"Why did you attack us, Mr. Bothwell?" Alexa asked.

"Didn't know who you were. I thought you were coming to rob the place, or else you were Violet back to do a clean job of killin' everyone." The old man hiccupped.

"We're not going to hurt you, Mr. Bothwell," Alexa said. "But we need to find Violet. She's going to kill my brother, and we need to stop her. Can you help us?"

"I don't think so, miss. I'm sorry. I wasn't much to stand up to her before. I'm not going anywhere near her now," he said.

"Can you at least tell us what happened?" Duster said.

He shrugged. "I imagine so. But I don't know what good it's going to do," Bothwell said.

Duster and Alexa helped the old man to his feet, and he led them down the stairs and into an ornate dining room that was in reasonably good shape compared with the rest of the house.

142

They sat at the long table. There were still plates with moldy pieces of food on them. Duster swiped the plate in front of him out of the way as he sat.

The old man hurriedly began picking up the dishes. "I'm sorry about this mess. I haven't been in this room since the day it happened," Bothwell said.

"Mr. Bothwell, don't worry about the dishes. Please just tell us what happened," Alexa said patiently.

"Well, one day, this woman come to the door. She was old, mind you. Older than me. She had brought a basket with her, and asked to speak to Mr. Wilks. I asked her what her business was, and she said that Mr. Wilks had met her in his travels and that he'd invited her. I thought she was telling the truth, because part of the magic of this house is that no one can find it unless they're told where it is. That's part of the enchantment that Mr. Wilks put on the house."

Alexa looked at Duster and he nodded. This explained why Duster had never seen the house before.

The old man plunged on. "So I went upstairs to tell him about the old woman. He didn't say anything, but I thought he seemed a little uneasy as he came down the stairs with me. He greeted her kindly. Mr. Wilks was a kind man, ya see. He was always gracious to his guests. He invited her into the study. They sat there in silence for a while. The old lady was watching me the whole time I was fixing them drinks. Then all of sudden, she asked Mr. Wilks if they could talk alone.

"Mr. Wilks said, 'of course' and dismissed me from the room. But I had a bad feeling about the way she'd been watching me. As soon as I closed the door behind me, I went around to the bedroom and listened through the door that connects it to the study.

"I heard Mr. Wilks ask the old lady who she was and where

she was from. She said her name was Violet, and she had a mountain keep just a few miles to the north. Then he asked her how she'd found the house. It was then that I knew there was going to be trouble. If Mr. Wilks hadn't invited her, she must be a powerful sorceress to break the enchantment.

"She seemed to ignore the question, and said that she'd been looking for Mr. Wilks for many years. That she had a secret to share with him. Mr. Wilks didn't say anything for a while.

"Finally, Mr. Wilks asked her what the secret was.

"The old lady said, 'I know how to use the magic without it draining my life.' Mr. Wilks didn't say anything to this. I remember thinking that the old lady's life looked pretty drained already.

"So he says, 'Why tell me?' Which you have to admit was a fair question. It's not like she knew Mr. Wilks.

"So Violet says that she knows it won't help her much any more because she's already so old, but that she's looking to preserve the lives of young sorcerers. Mr. Wilks didn't say anything to this. So finally, Violet asked Mr. Wilks if he had a family. Mr. Wilks told her yes, a wife and two children. Then she asked if any of them were sorcerers.

"Mr. Wilks laughed then. He said, 'Sorry to disappoint you, but I'm the only magician here. My wife comes from a family of bakers, and neither my son nor my daughter has shown even the slightest evidence that they inherited the power.'

"Violet asked how old the children were. I could tell Mr. Wilks didn't like that question. I could hear him shift in his seat. All he said was, "Old enough."

"They sat in silence for a few moments, and then Mr. Wilks asked the old lady if she required anything for her journey home. He didn't want to be rude, but Mr. Wilks was trying to get rid of her.

"Then she laughed. It was a horrible sound. It sounded like a creaking hiss. When I heard a glass hit the floor, the old lady was still laughing. I opened the door and saw the old woman from the back. She was standing with her hands raised, and Mr. Wilks was slumped in his chair like he couldn't move, but his eyes were wide with fear. I ran past the old lady and went to him. I asked him what happened, but he couldn't answer me. His eyes darted toward Violet and I turned to her and said, 'What did you do to him?'

"And she just laughed. Suddenly, I felt myself lifted off the ground and out the door until I was at the top step, and then the power holding me ended and I fell, toppling down the stairs. It was a miracle I didn't break my neck, but it knocked me out. Violet must have thought I was dead.

"When I woke up, I was still at the bottom of the stairs. It was dark. I got up. My ribs were on fire. I figured I broke a few of them. They're still not quite right." The old man stretched himself absentmindedly. "Then I went to look for everyone, and they were dead. Each of them. My mistress was on the floor in the kitchen. The children were slumped over at the table right here in this dining room. She must've killed them while they ate their lunch."

Duster glanced at the plate of food he'd shoved away with a look of renewed horror.

"I went to the kitchen and took out the biggest knife I could find, then hobbled back upstairs. My head was on fire. I listened at the top of the stairs and could hear a voice from one of the children's bedrooms. I walked over and I saw her, standing at the side of the bed. Mr. Wilks was lying in the bed, still not moving.

"Then I heard her say, 'The secret is this: to use the power without consequence, I take the magic of others and it sustains

145

my own power, my own life.' Then she started to do her spell. I watched in horror. I couldn't move. Then she reached down and touched Mr. Wilks on the head and he screamed. That sort of woke me up. I ran forward and plunged the knife into her back. She fell to her knees. I thought I'd killed her. Then I ran to Mr. Wilks, but he was already dead. His eyes were open. I could still see the shock on his face.

"Then I heard her behind me. She started for the door, and I turned to chase her. I was going to pick her up and throw her down the stairs with my bare hands!"

Alexa looked up at Duster, but he was transfixed by the old man. When Alexa looked back at Bothwell, he looked deranged with anger and grief.

"I took two steps, and she spun around and a blast of fire came out of her hand at me. That's how I got this." He waved his hand at the burn across his forehead. "But most of it missed me. It hit the bed and the whole thing went up in flames. I couldn't even get to Mr. Wilks's body." The old man took one long moment to breathe. "Once I put the fire out she was long gone."

Alexa and Duster stared at the man for a long while. He put his hands over his ears. It gave Duster and Alexa the impression that Bothwell was trying to hold his head together.

Alexa was still staring at the old man when Duster spoke. "That's what she's going to do to Michael."

Alexa stood up. "No, she's not."

Duster turned to look at her, but she was staring at the old man.

"Mr. Bothwell? Can we look around the house?"

The old man looked up, tears streaked his face. "Yes, my dear, but don't go in the cellar. I put the bodies there. I just couldn't bear to look at them. I put them there until I was strong enough to bury them."

They found the scene that Bothwell had described in one of the children's rooms. The charred remains of a man were on a burned bed. The walls were blackened, and there was a trail of blood on the carpeting.

In the cellar there were the bodies of a beautiful woman, her youthful face unmarked by care or worry, and two children. The boy looked to be about twelve. He had shoulder length hair and his lip was cut. His eyebrows were singed and his hand was badly burned. The girl, who looked to be about Alexa's age, had wavy black hair that was tied into a plait. Her skin was smooth, with a streak of green across her cheek. Alexa saw in her mind's eye this beautiful young girl putting a spoon to her lips when she was hit by Violet's spell. She imagined the boy, who had just watched his sister be killed, trying to fight or run away when Violet had killed him.

Duster put his hand on Alexa's shoulder. She stood stoically before the bodies of Violet's victims, shaking her head. She turned to Duster. "We have to stop her. Not just for Michael. These people didn't deserve this," she said.

Duster nodded. "We will."

Just a few minutes later, Duster and Alexa found themselves back in the forest, plunging through the thicket heading toward the road Duster said headed into the mountain range in the north.

"We're going to have to make camp soon," Duster said as he walked alongside of her. Alexa looked over. She could barely make out Duster's shape in the evening darkness.

"You're right," she said. "I'm sorry I turned the old man down when he asked us to stay there. I just couldn't do it. I couldn't stay there knowing what she did to those poor people."

"It's okay. I couldn't stay there, either." Duster turned

back in the direction of the house, which was already obscured by the trees and the night. "That poor old man shouldn't stay there, either. He's going to go crazy in there."

"Where else does he have to go?" Alexa asked.

Duster didn't respond. After a few minutes, he said, "Well, what did we learn there?"

Alexa had been thinking about it the whole way from the house, and she ticked off her answer as if she was reading from a prompt board. "Violet told Mr. Wilks that she had a mountain keep in the north. That's as good a guess as any as to where her lair might be. We also know that she had to do something to Mr. Wilks in order to keep him from fighting her, but to keep him alive until she could take his magic. But I don't know what."

She heard Duster breathe sharply. "The drink," he said. "Remember Bothwell told us that he heard the glass hit the floor, and then when he went in there, Wilks couldn't move. Maybe she used some sort of poison to keep Mr. Wilks from fighting her before she took his magic."

"Maybe," Alexa said. "We also know that she's vulnerable when she's casting her spell. That was the only time she was in any real danger. Bothwell might've killed her with the knife. It probably takes all of her focus and energy to perform that spell."

They walked in silence for a little while longer. Finally, when they stopped to set up camp for the night, Alexa said, "It's not much to go on. But it's a start."

CHAPTER 11
THE WOLF'S CHILDREN

The next morning Duster and Alexa started early, eating a meager breakfast of stale bread and blueberries. The day was overcast, with patches of drizzle creating mist as they trudged through the forest. Once they reached the village of Coyne, they skirted around it. Alexa thought that it was unlikely that anyone would remember them in the village, but Duster insisted that they avoid it anyway.

"Why take any chances?" he said.

They headed a little farther north than they had gone last time, and it was very slow going. The path was overgrown with heavy brush as they headed toward the mountain range another day's journey beyond.

Just after noon, they came upon another clearing with a smaller, walled village in the distance.

"I think that's Haventown," Duster said.

"I've never been there," Alexa said.

"It's been years, but I think my mother and I passed through here when we first came to Mr. Eckerly's farm looking for work. Maybe that was a different village. I don't remember

149

there being walls around it," Duster said.

They approached cautiously, looking around off into the trees on either side of them as they came closer to the gate. The walls of the city were made of wood, tied together with heavy ropes. They were many scorch marks and places where the wood had been scraped or cracked. There was a small wooden turret in one corner. Alexa could see a dark shape in a chair up there, but it didn't seem to be moving.

As they approached, Alexa saw the shape move. A man in a dark colored tunic and pants leaned over and slapped the railing of the turret, trying to gain the attention of someone below him. Alexa heard a faint whistling sound, and in a moment, the gate before them opened and four horses rushed through and were bearing down on them, a heavily armored knight on each horse. Three of them held swords, and the fourth dropped the heavily spiked head of a morning star out as he rode.

Alexa and Duster stopped and watched them approach, in shock that their appearance had caused such a swift and aggressive reaction.

"What should we do?" Alexa said, her eyes still on the riders.

"Nothing. They won't hurt us. We didn't do anything," Duster said, but his wide eyes belied the confidence of his words as he watched the riders.

Instinctively, Alexa put her hands up—so did Duster.

Only a few yards from them, the riders came to an abrupt halt. One of the men with a sword rode a few steps past the others, and shouted at them in a deep, crackling voice.

"Who are you and why have you come here?"

The man's helmet was inclined toward Duster, but he turned to face Alexa as she spoke. "I am Alexa Flynn. I'm from the Eckerly farm to the south. My brother and I are traveling to visit our grandparents."

"That is a lie," the knight said. His horse stamped angrily. "There are no villages through this way. There is nothing until well beyond the mountain range."

"Our grandparents live beyond the mountain range," Alexa said. She still had her hands up.

"You are lying, girl. We know what you are." The knight turned to his companions. "Bring them in," he said.

The other riders circled around Alexa and Duster. One of the knights reached down and grabbed Duster's pack and twisted it off his back. The group then headed to the gate. It opened quickly to allow them in, and was closed by two knights right after the last rider came through.

"Where are we going?" Alexa asked.

The rider made no response but led them on through a small town square. The buildings were squat, poorly constructed wooden flats. There were many walls where Alex and Duster could see large gaps between the timbers, and there were a few buildings with gaping holes in their ceilings. It looked as though the buildings in this town had been constructed very quickly, and by people without much skill in carpentry.

Many haggard and dirty faces peeked out of windows and doors to watch the procession walk down the main street. There were rumblings, and Alexa and Duster heard the sounds of some doors being bolted and windows being shut abruptly after they passed.

The knights led them to a small stone building, one of the only ones in the town. Alexa realized what it must be from the bars set into the windows.

"Why are you imprisoning us? We've committed no crime," she said. The rider behind her had dismounted and shoved her forward with the flat of his sword.

151

"Hey!" Duster turned to step between Alexa and the knight, but the knight brought the hilt up into Duster's face and he fell to his knees in the dirt.

"Stop! Don't hurt him!" Alexa screamed.

The knight dragged Duster back into a standing position and turned him around. The other knights had also dismounted, and they pushed them roughly into the jail building.

Inside the building there was a chair and table for a guard, and then a large cell with the one barred window Alexa had seen from the outside. The floor inside the jail was dirt.

Two prisoners in the cell, small boys, maybe nine or ten years old, stood up from where they'd been sitting on the cell floor near the door and backed into a corner.

One of the knights took a long key from an iron rung on the wall and unlocked the cell. Alexa and Duster were pushed inside and the door was quickly locked behind them. Another knight dropped Duster's pack on the floor next to the table.

Duster fell to his knees again in the cell. There was blood rushing from his nose and he was swaying as he knelt. Alexa thought he might pass out. She put her hands on his shoulders to steady him and said slowly, "Duster! Duster, look at me! You're okay."

For a few moments Alexa thought he might collapse, but then his eyes cleared a little and he sat down on the ground. "I'm all right," he said, waving his hand to show Alexa he didn't need her to hold him up any more. "I just want to sit for a minute until my head clears."

The knights had disappeared. Alexa went to the bars and yelled toward the door, "Why are we here? What's going on?"

Alexa had forgotten about the two young boys who were in the cell when they were led in. She turned as one of them spoke. "They think you are the wolf's children," he said.

152

He was a gangly boy, with dirt on his cheeks, and there were streaks in the dirt made by tears. He had filthy, matted hair that might've been black or brown—Alexa couldn't tell. There was a gap in his front teeth.

His companion was a little smaller than he was. Alexa could tell he had fairer skin, but he was just as dirty. His hair was a dusty color that Alexa thought meant that he was blond when it was clean. The smaller boy looked as if he'd been deflated— like he'd lost a great deal of weight in a short period of time.

"What?" Alexa said, taking a step forward.

The boys were sitting again, this time in the corner of the cell. The smaller one was pushing the dirt into small mounds around his feet and then kicking them down.

The older boy sat, his hands in his lap, staring up at Alexa. His eyes were of an icy blue, and Alexa saw dark rings around them.

"Are you the wolf's children?" he asked.

"I don't understand what you're talking about," Alexa said.

"We are. We helped to burn down the town last month," he said matter-of-factly.

"Why would you do that?" Alexa asked.

"Mother told us to," said the smaller boy, still looking down at the little mounds of dirt he was gathering together before himself. Then the smaller boy whispered to the older one. Alexa thought she heard him say he was hungry, but she couldn't be sure. The older boy shook his head at him.

It was then that the door opened and one of the knights reentered and stood next to the entrance at attention. Behind him came a man of about fifty, with silver hair and a short beard. He was dressed in a maroon tunic and tan pants. There was fine gold chain around his neck.

The man stopped before the cell. His voice was a rasping

bark. "I am Eldridge, Lord of Haventown. Who are you?" he demanded.

Alexa glanced back at the two boys on the floor; both had their heads down. She turned back toward the imposing man before her.

"I am Alexa Flynn. This is my brother, Duster—"

Eldridge cut her off. "I'm told that you are traveling through dangerous lands to your grandparents' house. I know that is a lie! No one travels through the Valley of the Wolf to visit relatives."

Alexa looked down at Duster, who was struggling to his feet. She reached out and helped pull him up. He stood next to Alexa, looked at the man through the bars, and then whispered, "I think we're going to have to tell him."

Alexa nodded. "Those are our names, but we're not brother and sister. We are from the Eckerly farm, and we travel north to find the keep of the crimson lady, a witch named Violet, who has taken my brother Michael. We seek to rescue him and destroy her."

Lord Eldridge considered them for a moment. He looked back and forth between Duster and Alexa. He looked down at their clothes, and then he studied Alexa thoughtfully.

"I know Mr. Eckerly. He used to travel through our city as a younger man, bartering his crops for metals, tools, and the like," Lord Edridge said. "I remember he always looked for exotic varieties of—"

"Barley," Duster said. "For the wheat beer he brews. The stuff is awful."

Lord Eldridge laughed. "He used to bring it to us as a gift for the midsummer festival. Barrels of it. The stuff was awful," he said. He turned to the knight who was still standing at attention at the door. "Arlon, let them out."

The knight came forward quickly and unlocked the door. Alexa and Duster walked out. As Lord Eldridge beckoned them forward, Alexa asked, "What will happen to them?" indicating the two boys still in the cell.

Lord Eldridge shook his head wearily. "We're not sure what to do with them. Normally we execute the wolf's children when we catch them, but these are so young."

"You execute children?" Duster said.

"They're not really children," said Lord Eldridge, his face reddening with anger. "They do the bidding of the she-wolf, Camara, who has been a plague to our village for several years. Before, however, it was just her prowling around the village at night, attacking livestock or the occasional traveler who happened to be out alone at night. For a year she has been coming into the town accompanied by humans calling themselves her children. Dozens of them—like those filthy mongrels in that cell. They are like animals themselves—savages who eat human flesh. Most of them are a little older than that, though. About two months ago, she arrived with the largest force of children we'd ever seen, near thirty, and they burned down Haventown. Many of our people were killed. So forgive me if I don't show those children any mercy."

Alexa thought about the small boy whispering to his companion about being hungry, and shuddered.

Lord Eldridge led them outside. "We came as far as we could, to this edge of the valley, and built this shanty town." He waved his arm before him to indicate the cluster of buildings around the town square. "We'll live here until we can return to the village of our ancestors and rebuild it."

"But I don't understand. Where has the wolf found these children? How does she control them? Those little boys in that cell are convinced that the wolf is their mother. How did that

155

happen?" Alexa said.

"I don't have any answers," Lord Eldridge said. Suddenly, he looked away from her. "To be honest with you, I don't care. All I want is to destroy this dog and her litter, and return my people to their homes." Lord Eldridge stopped in the middle of the square and turned to them. "I'm sorry," he said. "I'm sorry you were imprisoned and that you think me a heartless barbarian, but you don't understand what it's like to live under siege." He brushed his hand through his silver hair and sighed. He looked beaten. "I will not see Haventown destroyed on my watch." He looked into each of their faces. His eyes were a soft hazel.

Duster nodded. Alexa looked at Lord Eldridge without expression. She couldn't put the image of the small boys from her mind.

He led them to an inn off the town square. The weathered sign must have been brought with them from the original Haventown. It read "The Briar Inn." This building was larger and better constructed than the other buildings in the town. Like the jail, it was made of stone. The masonry was impeccable — the walls appeared perfectly straight, and there wasn't a single crack to be seen from the front. As they climbed the front steps, Alexa noticed that the floor consisted of many different types of timbers that had not been varnished yet, but that the floor was straight and there were no gaps between the boards. Alexa doubted that any of the other buildings had a floor like this.

When they entered there was a short bar, made of wood, behind which stood a tall barman with a sweeping black mustache. Alexa saw that he had huge hands, marked with calluses and scars, which were clasped before him on the bar. He leaned over the bar, talking quietly to a young woman in an apron. He was smiling fondly at her as she whispered to him. When he noticed Lord Eldridge leading in the strangers, he straightened up.

"Lord Eldridge, to what do I owe the pleasure?" The barman's soft voice stood in contrast to his imposing stature.

Lord Eldridge walked up to the bar and put his fist on it. "Karl, we require some of your wheat beer, and these two could use a meal," he said, jerking his head toward Alexa and Duster.

Karl looked at Duster and Alexa and smiled. "Chicken stew? It should be just about ready."

"Yes. Thank you," Alexa said.

Alexa looked over at the barmaid, who was a tall girl with curly red hair, to nod her thanks as well, but she saw that the barmaid had taken no notice of her. She was staring hungrily at Duster. The girl looked to be a year or two older than she was—about Duster's age, she figured—and the white blouse she wore was open at the top, exposing her soft skin.

Alexa immediately took a self-conscious look at her own tattered work shirt and frowned. She took a step back and slid her hand into Duster's. It was then that the barmaid seemed to notice her for the first time. She met Alexa's eyes, and quickly looked away.

Alexa glanced up at Duster, but he was looking off to the side of the bar where a large fireplace stood, an enormous iron pot boiling in the fire. As she turned, she smelled the hearty stew from across the room and her stomach rumbled loudly. She put her hand on her stomach and said, "Sorry."

The barman laughed quietly and said, "No need to apologize, miss. I'll get you a big bowl." Coming around the bar, he waved them to a table and said, "Get the beer," to the barmaid. Alexa, Duster, and Lord Eldridge sat as Karl hurried over to the fireplace.

"None for me," Lord Eldridge said as Karl placed a bowl of

steaming hot stew in front of him.

Karl placed a loaf of bread and bowls of stew in front of Duster and Alexa, and they began to eat with gusto.

"This is so good," Duster said through a mouthful. The barmaid came up and placed the mugs of wheat beer on the table before them. She turned the handle of Duster's so that it was near his hand. Duster said, "Thanks," and a little stew slid down his chin.

Alexa laughed and wiped his chin. She looked up and the barmaid had walked away, but she was looking over her shoulder sulkily.

Alexa took a drink from the heavy mug of beer. She puckered her lips a little at the bitterness, but the beer was smooth and icy cold. She liked the taste.

"Now that is beer," said Lord Eldridge, wiping his mouth with the back of his hand. "My apologies to Mr. Eckerly," he added, and Duster laughed.

"You are on a mission to rescue your brother?" Lord Eldridge said.

"Yes. The witch, Violet, has taken him to her keep in the mountains, and we need to get there...quickly," Alexa said.

"I've never heard of this witch. Are you certain that her keep is in the mountains?"

"Actually, no," Duster said. "But it's the only lead we have."

Lord Eldridge nodded slowly. Alexa thought he was deciding whether or not to tell them something.

"How far does the valley spread? Can we go around it to avoid the wolf?" she asked.

"You can, but if you would travel quickly, the valley is the only way. It stretches for miles in both directions, and then you'll have to scale the mountains to enter the range. To travel through the valley, you must journey due north into the wolf's lands, but there is a passage into the mountains on the other side. It is the quickest way — if you survive."

"Can you help us? Can you send some soldiers with us?" Duster said.

"I'm sorry," said Lord Eldridge. "I won't send any of my men to their deaths into the valley. This is your journey."

Alexa had known as soon as Duster asked the question what the response would be, but she still winced as Lord Eldridge pronounced their journey a death sentence.

"In any case, I wish you good luck," he said, rising from his chair and tossing coins on the table. Then he was gone, leaving Duster and Alexa alone to stare after him, the door still swinging behind him.

"He's so charming, isn't he?" asked Karl as he swept by to bring them another mug of wheat beer. "Would you like more to eat?"

Alexa shook her head. "No thank you. It was delicious."

"Yeah, it was," Duster said, leaning back in his chair, looking as though he might fall asleep right then and there.

Karl laughed quietly and his paunch quivered beneath his apron. "I'm glad you liked it. Will you require a room? Or two?" he asked, one eyebrow raised.

Alexa looked over at Duster, but he was so overcome after the stew and bread, he didn't seem to notice what the barman meant. "Oh no, sir. We'll be leaving shortly. We have a long way to travel yet today," she said to Karl.

"Then I wish you well on your journey. I will pack you some food if you would like before you go," he said, bowing graciously.

"Thank you so much," Duster said, and Alexa nodded fervently at his side.

A few minutes later, Duster and Alexa emerged into the

square again, and were about to head north when Duster suddenly stopped. "My pack. It's in the jail building," he said.

"Do we need it?" Alexa asked, holding up the bag that Karl had just packed for them. She was anxious to get going.

"It's got food, some supplies, and all my money in it. We need all the food we can get if we're heading into the mountains," he said.

Alexa nodded and they headed back toward the jail building.

When they reached it, Duster banged heavily on the wooden door. One of the knights who had captured them came and opened it.

"I need my pack," Duster said.

The knight nodded, rubbing sleep out his eyes, and stood back to let them enter. He closed the door behind them and went back to his chair. He put his feet up and closed his eyes. He was asleep instantly.

Duster and Alexa looked around, and then he saw his pack on the floor. He picked it up, put it on the table, and began looking through it to see if anything had been taken.

Meanwhile, Alexa saw the two boys still sitting on the ground in the cell. The smaller of the boys had his back against the wall and seemed to be sleeping. The older boy was sitting in the center, rocking back and forth, his arms hugging his knees. He was staring blankly at the bars before him.

"Have you eaten anything today?" she said.

The boy didn't seem to hear Alexa. He just kept rocking nervously.

"Hey," Alexa said a little louder.

The boy continued to rock, but his face rose to look into Alexa's.

"Have you eaten anything today?" she said again.

160

The boys shook his head. Alexa wondered if the jailor fed these boys at all.

Alexa rummaged through the bag of food and took out a small loaf of bread. They couldn't spare much with the journey before them, but Alexa couldn't bear to let them starve, no matter what they had done.

Alexa looked back and saw that the guard was clearly asleep, so she tossed the small loaf of bread through the bars. The boy shoved his companion's leg and then crawled over to the loaf of bread. The boy sniffed at the bread, like a dog would, before picking it up and tearing it in half. The other boy was still stretching when the older boy threw half of the bread to him and it landed in his lap.

The boys ate ferociously, grunting and sighing as they devoured the bread in seconds. Alexa was both disgusted and fascinated as she watched the boys eat. The older boy finished first, and picked crumbs off the dirt floor and ate them.

When the smaller boy finished, he said, "It was like Grandmother's bread."

Alexa came forward and stood at the bars. "Grandmother?" she said. "Your mother is a wolf. How can a wolf bake bread?"

The older boy spoke. "Grandmother is not a wolf. Grandmother is like us," he said.

"When we are with Mother, we hunt our food as wolves do. But when Grandmother visits us, she brings other food: bread, carrots, potatoes," the smaller boy said. "I like potatoes."

An idea burst into Alexa's head, and she was about to turn and wave Duster over, but he was already beside her. His eyes lit with recognition as he spoke. "What's your grandmother's name?" he asked.

"We just call her Grandmother," the smaller boy said.

"Well, what does she look like?" Alexa asked.

161

The older boy shrugged. "She's an old woman with stringy white hair."

"Is she tall?"

"She might be, but she's always hunched over," the older boy said.

"I like Grandmother's laugh," the smaller boy said. "It sort of sounds like—"

"Creaking," Alexa and Duster said together.

"Yes." The younger boy's eyes lit up. "I like when she makes the light for us, too," he said.

"What light?" Duster asked, but Alexa already knew.

"She can make pretty lights appear in her hands," the smaller boy said.

"And she can move things without touching them," the older boy added eagerly.

Alexa turned and walked away from the bars. It was a few moments before Duster realized that she was gone. Alexa was already out the door and walking briskly into the square again when Duster caught up with her.

"Hey, what's the matter?" he said.

"I know what we have to do," she said, her eyes forward. "We're going to help those boys escape."

CHAPTER 12
JEALOUSY AND JAILBREAK

Duster and Alexa spent the next several hours in the inn, huddled in a corner near the fire, discussing their plan.

They weren't worried about getting the boys out of the jail. Alexa thought that would be relatively easy. The guard had not taken them very seriously, and had slept through his watch while the boys were in the cell, even while Duster and Alexa had been there.

The real problem was the gate. They didn't know how they were going to get the guards to open it for them. When Duster asked Karl about it, Karl told him that they never open the gates at night. People simply weren't allowed to leave at night, and visitors who arrived after sunset would have to wait until morning to be allowed inside the gates, when they could be properly searched.

Duster had suggested trying to climb over the wall, but one trip out to inspect the high, sheer surface told them it would be too difficult—especially with the boys.

It wasn't until late in the afternoon when a solution presented itself. Duster came in from a walk outside with an embarrassed smile on his face.

"What?" Alexa said.

Suddenly the pretty red-haired waitress came in through the door, and she wore a similar, guilty looking grin. When she entered, the girl took a swift glance at Alexa and looked away, heading to the bar.

"I think I found us a way out," Duster said.

Alexa turned in her seat to look at the waitress as she tied her apron around the back. She was talking to Karl, but there was still a glowing smile on her face.

Alexa turned back and looked up at Duster. "How?" she said with as much malice as she could muster.

"Not here," Duster said, and nodded toward the door.

Alexa got up and followed him outside, giving one more glance to the waitress as she went.

Duster was walking slowly down the street, waiting for Alexa to catch up. He kept his eyes forward and his voice low as he spoke.

"The waitress—" he began.

"What about her?" Alexa said.

Duster turned to her, an amused smirk on his face. "Jealous?"

Alexa could feel her face flush, but she pretended to be calm. "What about her?" she said more casually.

Duster laughed. "She came up to me in the street and asked to meet me later."

Alexa's eyes narrowed and Duster plunged on quickly. "I started to tell her that you were my fiancée, and that you were the really jealous type, and that if I was missing tonight you would tear the town apart looking for me." He paused for a moment, and then added sheepishly, "You know, just to get her off my back."

"Where is that — ?" Alexa said, and she made to turn back toward the inn.

Duster grabbed her shoulder. "Just listen," he said.

Alexa looked back toward the inn one more time, but then looked up at Duster.

"So she told me that we could sneak outside the walls so that you wouldn't find us," Duster said.

Alexa stopped in her tracks. "What?"

Duster was beaming at her. "The waitress is Karl's daughter, and their house is right next to the wall on the east end of the town. Karl's a builder — I mean, look at The Briar Inn. It's the nicest building in town, right? So when they moved the town and put up the walls, Karl knew that Lord Eldridge and his knights would control the gates. If Karl wanted to bring anything in, the knights would inspect the wagons and probably take what they wanted. There'd be nothing that Karl could do about it. So Karl built a shed that's right against the wood, and cut a secret door into the wall, so that he can get deliveries without having to give anything to the knights. According to Trisa, Lord Eldridge knows he's getting supplies into the town under his nose, but he doesn't know how."

Alexa was still standing where she'd stopped, her brain working furiously. Suddenly she said, "Trisa?"

Duster rolled his eyes. "That's her name," he said, and Alexa nodded. "So once she told me all that, I told her I might be interested in one little fling before I got married." He raised his eyebrows in mock suavity, and Alexa laughed. Duster turned back toward the inn. "I'm pretty sure she's used that secret door for her little meetings before," he said.

"I guess we're lucky you're so good-looking," Alexa said, and started to walk away.

Duster laughed and followed her down the street.

165

***

An hour after sundown, Alexa stood face to face with the young waitress at the bar. "Can I help you?" Trisa said. Alexa noticed that she curled her lip in a tiny smile while she waited for Alexa's reply.

"Yes," Alexa answered formally. "As I'm sure you know, my fiancé and I were held in the jail this morning before Lord Eldridge determined that we were wrongfully imprisoned. We'd like to show the knights on guard that there are no hard feelings. We'd like to purchase a carafe of your best wine and send it over to them," she said. As she kept her face impassive, Alexa was flexing her knuckles under the bar where the waitress couldn't see.

"Sure. That'll be two silver," the waitress said, putting the carafe on the bar.

"Would you be so kind as to deliver it to them? There's another silver in it for you," Alexa said, holding up a handful of Duster's coins.

As she held out her hand, Trisa saw the half-moon bracelet on Alexa's wrist. The waitress looked up at Alexa. "That's pretty," she said.

"Oh. Thanks. It was a gift from Dust—I mean, it was a gift from my fiancé," Alexa said.

They stood in silence for a moment until Trisa took the coins out of Alexa's hand.

"Of course I'll take the wine, miss," the waitress said stiffly. Then she picked up the carafe and went out of the bar.

After the waitress left, Duster came to Alexa. "I'm sorry about your money," she said. "There's only a little left now."

"Don't worry about it. It's well worth it to make sure that you get in and out of that jailhouse without any trouble tonight." He reached up and lightly took a strand of hair that had fallen

166

into Alexa's face, and smoothed it behind her ear.

Alexa closed her eyes, waiting.

"It's almost time," Duster said.

"Yeah, it is."

Alexa opened her eyes and noticed that Duster was staring down at the half-moon bracelet and gently running his fingers over the charms. She reached up on her tiptoes and kissed Duster on the mouth. At first he stiffened in surprise, and then she felt him relax and put one hand on her back, and with the other he gently cradled her neck.

Alexa felt the warmth of his fingers and his lips and wanted to stay there forever. After a long moment, they broke apart and looked away from each other, both their faces flushed.

Not a moment too soon, either, as just then the waitress reentered the inn. She looked haughtily at them as she passed, and then disappeared into the back room.

"That might've blown the whole thing," Alexa said, the corners of her lips quirking in a smile. "If your little friend saw us and got mad at you...."

"Yeah," Duster said.

They walked back over to the table, and Alexa picked up both Duster's pack and the one Karl had given them.

"I'll meet you outside the walls in two hours," she said quietly. She headed to the door and looked over her shoulder. Duster gave her a wink and she turned out into the night.

Alexa was still smiling as she walked slowly through the square. She headed instinctively toward the east end of town, and walked past Karl's large house. Duster was right—Karl was quite the builder. His home and the inn were easily the most solid and symmetrical buildings in what had become Haventown. She walked far enough down the street to where she could make out the small shed Duster had described up against the wooden wall.

She walked through the square one more time, taking note where guards were stationed. There were only a few about, and even these were only strolling lazily through the streets. They weren't on alert for anything, and Alexa was glad for it.

After an hour, Alexa made her way to the jailhouse. She knocked on the heavy door and waited. No one answered. Then she knocked again, harder this time. A small feeling of panic rose in her as she imagined that the knight she'd expected to be drunk upon her arrival had passed out and would never open the door. It was just as this terrifying thought entered her mind that suddenly the door swung open, revealing a slovenly knight, his breastplate off, holding on to the door for support. He had a long face, like a horse, and a scruffy brown beard.

"What do you want?" he slurred.

"I've come to make sure you received our gift," she said.

"What? The wine? Oh yes," he said. "Much obliged." He hiccupped loudly. The sleepy-eyed knight had a large crimson stain on his shirt. He stepped back and looked Alexa up and down. "Would you like some? There's still a little left." He pointed at the carafe on the table.

"That would be lovely. Thank you," Alexa said, and walked inside as the knight bowed her into the room.

Alexa looked and saw the key on a heavy iron rung on the wall. The sleeping forms of the two little boys were curled up, much like pups, on the dirt floor of the cell. She stopped next to the table and turned toward the knight.

"Let me find a glass," he said as he stumbled forward into the room.

"There's no need," she said, and picked up the carafe. "To the guardians of Haventown," she said, and brought it to her lips. She let a little of the wine touch her lips, but let it go no further. She wanted the knight to finish the wine.

He bowed to her and took the carafe. "To your generosity," he said, and took a drink. "And to your beauty." He drained the rest of the wine.

The knight put the carafe down heavily on the table and stumbled.

"You should probably sit down," Alexa said, leading him over to his chair and pushing him into it. The knight rocked dangerously and nearly fell off. Then he sat, staring forward for a few moments, until his eyes drooped and his head sagged against his chest. It would only be another moment now.

Alexa stood rooted to the spot, waiting for the knight's eyes to close. She could feel the sweat on her palms as she waited. She didn't dare move.

After a minute that seemed an eternity, the knight's eyes closed. His mouth opened and he began to snore.

Alexa waved her hand in front of his face, just to be sure he was out, and then walked as silently as she could toward the key on the wall. She lifted it, careful not to let it scrape on its iron rung, and went quickly over to the cell. She turned the key and the lock clicked open. It seemed so loud in the silence of the jail. She looked back at the knight, but he was still dozing. Alexa swung the gate open slowly and went into the cell. She knelt next to the two boys and shook them gently.

The older boy's eyes opened immediately and he stared at Alexa, but didn't say anything. The younger boy stretched himself on the floor and started to groan before opening his eyes. Alexa slapped her hand over his mouth. His eyes flew open and he looked at her in confusion.

"I'm going to help you escape from here and bring you back to your mother," she whispered. "You have to be really quiet and do what I say."

169

The boys looked at each other, and then the older boy nodded.

They all walked out of the cell. Alexa closed it gently behind her, but didn't bother locking it. They walked past the drunken guard, each watching him as they stepped toward the heavy door.

Just as Alexa came to the door, it was pushed open. Two knights in a whispered conversation stood on the doorstep, and were about to enter.

Everyone stood completely still for a moment, taking in what was happening. It was the first knight who reached for the sword at his side and yelled, "Escape!" Alexa ran forward and barreled into him as he struggled to get the sword out in the tight space of the doorway.

His companion, who was a little behind, had his vision blocked and didn't see Alexa rush forward. The knights were knocked backwards and Alexa yelled, "Come on!" The older boy grabbed the younger one by the arm and thrust him through the door. Alexa grabbed his chubby hand and pulled him behind her, and reached out as the older boy ran forward.

Just then, the lead knight had gotten his sword free and raised it to strike the boy as he passed. Alexa rushed forward and grabbed the knight's arms. She raised him off the ground and threw him twenty feet into the wall of the next building. The knight hit the wall, slid down to the ground, and moved no more.

Alexa turned in shock and found the other knight, his sword drawn, staring at her in amazement.

Alexa took the opportunity and grabbed each boy by the hand and ran. She glanced back and saw the knight watch her for a moment, and then rush to the aid of his companion, still crumpled against the wall.

170

Alexa pulled the two boys forward until they could keep up with her on their own. The plan had been to go stealthily through the town until they reached the shed, but Alexa knew they didn't have much time now. They ran full out, not worrying about the noise or if anyone saw them. They had to get to the shed behind Karl's house.

As they turned down the street, Alexa had a horrifying thought: if Duster hadn't already gone through the shed with the waitress, they were doomed.

It was while they were running flat out down the darkened street that they heard the alarm being raised. The guard in the tower on the south end of town blew a horn and shouted, "Escape! Escape!"

When she reached Karl's house, Alexa ran past to the edge of it and hid, waiting for the two boys. They came tearing around the corner and stopped beside her in the shadows. The older boy took two deep, panting breaths and then blurted out, "How did you do that? You threw him like a rag doll!"

Alexa knew there was no time to answer questions. She put her finger to her lips and dared to look out into the street. Five or six knights were in the square dividing up areas to search. Another one came stumbling out of the shadows and was clumsily putting on his armor. Alexa couldn't tell if that was the drunken guard she'd left at the jail or if it was a different knight roused out of bed by the alarm.

They crept noiselessly down the side of Karl's house. Alexa was certain that Karl wouldn't be home because he'd be at the inn, but she didn't know if Karl was married or had any other children.

Alexa and the boys crawled along the side of the house so that they weren't visible in the windows, and when they came to the edge of the house they saw the large open space they'd

171

have to cross to get to the shed without anyone seeing them.

They also had to hope that Duster and Trisa had already gone through and left the door unlocked.

Alexa got to her feet—so did the boys. They ran quickly and quietly through the open space and reached the shed. No one screamed in alarm, so Alexa hoped they'd gone unnoticed and grabbed the handle of the shed and it opened. She ushered the boys inside and followed after them. She closed the door quietly behind her.

The shed was a small, wooden structure, and when Alexa closed the door, it was as black as pitch inside. She whispered quietly, "There's a door here somewhere. Over here." She patted the east wall, hoping that the boys could tell by the sound where she was.

She could hear the boys feeling around on the wall like she was, and she bumped into one of them, knocking him to the ground.

"Sorry," Alexa whispered, not knowing which boy it was.

Suddenly there was a click, and Alexa recognized the voice of the older boy. "I think I've got it." Then there was a creaking sound, and they could feel the night air as the door opened out through the wall. They walked through and Alexa pushed it close behind her until she heard it click. It was hard to see in the dark anyway, but she couldn't make out the outline of the door at all. It was extremely well hidden.

They could still hear the commotion behind the wall as guards searched for them in vain. There was no tower on the eastern end for a guard to look down on them, and Alexa was thankful for that. As Alexa turned she saw the ground sloping downward into the woodlands. Before she moved, she listened for any sound of Duster and Trisa.

She thought she could hear the slightest rustling of leaves

a little way before her. She touched each of the boys on the shoulder and motioned that they should walk down into the valley. They nodded. Alexa began to walk carefully, making sure not to trip on brambles or step on leaves as best she could. The boys followed.

They reached the edge of the forest and Alexa thought she could make out a light before her. They walked quietly toward it. As they got nearer, they heard voices.

Alexa heard Trisa's voice echo a little too loudly. "Well why did you want to meet me out here if you didn't want to do anything?"

"Listen," she heard Duster whisper, "I just can't do it, okay?"

Alexa wondered how long Duster had been trying to stall the waitress while he waited for them. She turned to the boys and handed each of them one of the packs she had been carrying since she left the inn. She whispered, "Stay behind the trees and don't come out till she's gone."

The two boys moved quietly to where Alexa indicated.

Then Alexa drew herself up to her full height and stalked out into the small clearing where Duster and Trisa sat on a rock in front of a small fire.

"What are you doing here?" Alexa said quietly, but as fiercely as she could.

Duster leapt to his feet in partially feigned and partially real shock. "Nothing. I wasn't doing anything. I was just—"

But Alexa stomped over to where the waitress sat. As she approached, Trisa stood up and faced her. "What do you think we were doing?" Trisa said.

Alexa tried to be as imposing as she could, but it was hard because she only came up to Trisa's chin. "You stay away from my fiancé."

Trisa looked Alexa up and down again, just like she had in the bar. Alexa watched the tall waitress flex her knuckles. She was sure Trisa was deciding whether or not Duster was worth fighting for. Trisa looked over at Duster and snorted. "You two deserve each other," she said, and shoving past Alexa, she huffed away toward the secret door in the wall.

Alexa and Duster stood in silence until they were sure Trisa was gone, and then Alexa ran back to the trees and found the boys, rummaging through the packs and eating a loaf of bread Karl had given them.

She grabbed the packs from them and pulled them forward. "You can't eat this all now. We need it for the journey," she said.

When they came back into the clearing Duster had put out the fire, and they hurried away from the danger of Haventown and into the dangers of the Valley of the Wolf.

CHAPTER 13
THE VALLEY OF THE WOLF

Duster, Alexa, and the two boys traveled quickly through the woods of the valley. The older boy, Webb, knew his way. He ran almost as fast as a wolf, too. He hunched over and pulled himself forward with his hands as he took short, quick steps.

The younger boy, Fawn, ran in the same awkward fashion, but wasn't as fast and didn't have the endurance that Webb had.

Alexa and Duster struggled to keep up as the wolf-boys led them through almost perfect darkness around great trees, with trunks as wide as houses, through slimy marshes covered in algae, and over rocky, uneven ground as if they were used to traveling with a master cracking a whip at their backs.

And just as Alexa felt that she could go no further—when the sun tinged the horizon a shocking orange—Webb announced that they would reach the wolf's home in an hour.

Alexa fell to the grass and lay on her back, panting for breath. Duster, who was used to hard labor in the fields, was bent double, his hands on his knees, looking rather green after the hard night's journey.

"You must rest," Webb announced, although he didn't even appear winded by the breakneck pace of the trek.

Fawn sat on the ground next to Alexa, and as she looked over at him, he at least showed signs of heavy perspiration on his forehead and through his tattered, formless shirt.

"Now will you tell us how you threw the man?" Fawn asked, looking beseechingly at Alexa.

Alexa thought back to the moment when the guard had attempted to bring his sword down on Webb as they tried to escape. She thought about her immediate reaction to grab on to the knight just to protect the boy, and the immense power she'd felt in her limbs as she picked him up and flung him away.

How could she explain that to them? Alexa wasn't sure that she could explain it to herself. Finally, she said, "Sometimes when I'm scared that someone is going to hurt me or my friends, I get this power that protects us." Alexa thought about it, and decided that she was telling the most honest truth she could.

"Can you control your powers — like Grandmother?" Webb asked.

"Not really. She has studied a long time. She knows how to use her power. I don't," Alexa said.

"Maybe she will teach you," said Fawn, hopefully.

"I seriously doubt that," Alexa said.

"It must be wonderful to have the power to protect people like that. No one you love can ever be hurt," Webb said. His eyes shone in admiration.

But after Webb spoke, Alexa felt a welling sadness that started in her chest, and she quickly found herself wiping tears from her eyes. She saw her mother's body lying face down on the floor of their house, a dark stain spreading on her back.

"It doesn't always work," she said.

Duster came to her and put his hand on Alexa's shoulder.

"So tell us about your grandmother," Duster said. "What kind of things can she do with her power?"

Webb shrugged. "Like we told you, she can move stones around without touching them; she makes lights appear in the sky — mostly stuff like that."

"She can hurt Mother," Fawn said quietly.

"Shut up," Webb said.

"What do you mean? How does she hurt your mother?" Duster said.

Fawn looked at Webb. They boys stared at each other in silence.

Duster repeated the question. Finally, Webb turned away.

Fawn spoke, "She can make Mother scream and cry. I hate it."

"I don't understand. What does she do to her?" Alexa asked, but Fawn just shook his head.

"I always ask Mother about it, and she always tells me to leave her alone. But one time, right after Grandmother had been there and had been angry and made Mother scream, she told me that Grandmother can make her see things in her head. Terrible things," Webb said.

"What things?" Duster asked.

"I don't know. She wouldn't say."

Webb and Fawn walked upright, leading Duster and Alexa slowly in the last few miles of their journey to wolf's den. Even though the boys had no reason to be afraid, they seemed to sense Duster and Alexa's fear and let them slow the pace.

"What will happen when you take us to Mother?" Webb asked.

"What do you mean?" Alexa said, surprised by the question.

"What will you ask her for?" Fawn said.

"How do you know we're going to ask her for something?"

Duster said.

"There is no reason for you to rescue us and to bring us back unless you want something from Mother," Webb said.

Alexa was impressed at the shrewdness of the wolf boys, but for some reason, it made her sad, too. "We're going to ask for her help," Alexa said.

"Help with what?" Fawn asked.

Duster shook his head at Alexa. Alexa stared into Webb and Fawn's eager faces and sighed. "I don't know if I can tell you. It's something I have to ask your mother."

"Mother doesn't like secrets," Webb said darkly, walking ahead of them.

The sun was up completely when they reached the mouth of a large cave at the foot of the mountain. Webb and Fawn ran forward toward the cave. Alexa made to follow, but Duster grabbed her hand and held her back.

"This isn't going to work," he said. "We should get out of here."

"What choice do we have?" Alexa said. "Besides, Camara is their mother. She'll be grateful we brought them back." She looked quickly away from him into the cave. She didn't want Duster to see that she wasn't quite as confident as she sounded.

Duster came forward and stood next to Alexa. He took her hand in his and they faced the mouth of the cave. After a few seconds, children started to come out and scatter around them. They were all dirty and feral-looking, like Webb and Fawn. Most appeared to be thirteen or fourteen, but Alexa was sure that one tall boy with a patchy beard was at least as old as she was. The children eyed Duster and Alexa suspiciously, but didn't move toward them. They just stood by, watching.

Then Webb and Fawn came out of the cave, and Alexa saw a deepening of the shadows as the cave's mouth was filled with the largest gray wolf she had ever seen.

Camara came out into the mouth of the cave—her gnarled head was almost as large as Fawn's entire body. There was a patch of pink flesh visible where the fur had been cut or burned, and Camara's muzzle was spotted with specks of blood.

Alexa wondered if Camara had just eaten, or if the blood had permanently stained her fur.

Webb and Fawn stood on either side of the cave mouth. Both looked out at Duster and Alexa impassively as their mother spoke. The voice of he she-wolf was a low growl that Alexa had to strain to hear clearly.

"Thank you for freeing my sons and bringing them back to me."

"You're welcome," Alexa said.

"Now, Webb tells me that you will ask for my help. What is it that you would ask of me?" she snarled.

"Can we speak privately?" Alexa said.

Camara snorted, a low, guttural sound, and Alexa realized that it must be a laugh.

"Whatever you would ask, you may ask before my sons and daughters," she said.

Duster bent quickly and whispered, "Let's just forget it."

Alexa shook her head and put her hands on her hips to keep the she-wolf from seeing them shake. "Fine. We have risked our lives to bring you your children. Now I ask that you bring us to the keep of the crimson lady in the mountains. She has kidnapped my brother, and I want to save him."

Suddenly the she-wolf lunged forward from the cave. Her body was a tangle of sleek gray fur and muscle, larger than a horse. She reared up on her hind legs, and Alexa covered her face with her hands while Duster pressed his body against hers, steeling himself for the attack.

But it never came. When they looked, Camara stood just a few feet in front of them, her fierce black eyes staring into their frightened faces. She stalked a few steps back and forth, clawing the ground. Her haunches writhed like enormous serpents as she circled Duster and Alexa. They both turned with the wolf, unwilling to allow her behind them.

"What you ask is impossible," she said.

Alexa broke free from Duster's grip. "Why?"

"You do not know the crimson lady as I do. She is a witch of great power. If she has taken your brother, he is as good as dead," she said.

"You don't understand —" Alexa began.

"I understand perfectly. I cannot bring you to the crimson lady. Our arrangement is that I protect her lands, not bring her enemies within it."

"Your arrangement? What about the lives of your children?" Alexa said.

"That is the only reason you are still alive," the wolf said. "You must leave now."

Alexa looked quickly at Webb, and he gave her the slightest, almost imperceptible nod. Alexa recognized the fear etched into his features, and knew there was nothing that she could say that would change Camara's mind.

"Come on, Alexa," Duster said, pulling her away from the wolf.

They backed away slowly, careful not to trip as they headed toward the woods.

They walked in silence for several minutes. Alexa felt tears stinging her eyes, but she refused to wipe them. She knew that it was only a matter of time before she broke down. The farther they walked, the more she felt that Michael was already dead — and so was her father.

180

Alexa was yanked out of the spiral of despair when Duster suddenly grabbed her arm. He put his finger to his lips and nodded back in the general direction of the Camara's cave.

They traveled slowly and as silently as they could. Duster led her in a wide arc around the clearing before the cave entrance, and it was then that Alexa finally understood that Duster meant to hide in the woods just to the west of the cave mouth, within just a few hundred yards of it, but far enough away that they couldn't be seen or, as Alexa feared, smelled by the she-wolf or her children.

Once they found a small rise in the brush where they could sit comfortably and see out toward the cave, they settled in to wait for nightfall. They spoke very little throughout the rest of the day, fearing that Camara's children might keep watch on the area and hear their voices.

It was a couple of hours later, after Duster had made another quick search of the area and found no one around, that he finally explained to Alexa what he had in mind.

"If it's Camara's job to guard the lands from people trying to approach Violet's keep, she's going to send a messenger to her. Probably at night to avoid detection. We've got to keep a lookout, and when we see that messenger we can sneak out and try to follow him," he said, still warily scanning the area.

Alexa could think of no other way they might find their way to Violet's keep, so she nodded.

They kept watch well into the night, and not one of Camara's children came out of the cave. It was sunrise when Alexa, both physically and emotionally exhausted, gave up hope that Camara would send her messenger.

By this time, it had been three days and nights since Violet carried Michael off. Alexa knew there was only a slim chance that he was still alive.

Then suddenly, as if she materialized out of thin air, the stooped figure of the crimson lady appeared on the path beyond the cave and came plodding slowly along, bent over a walking stick.

One of Camara's daughters, a girl that Duster had heard Fawn call Misha, ran to her and embraced her. As the girl ran back toward the cave, she called back over her shoulder. "I can't wait to tell Mother you're here," she said.

Alexa pulled the kitchen knife from her belt and went to move nearer the cave to get to Violet, but Duster grabbed her hand and wouldn't relinquish it.

"This may be our only chance," she said through gritted teeth, but Duster shook his head.

"They'll kill us. There's too many of them," he said.

As Camara and a dozen of her children came out of the cave, Alexa knew he was right. That didn't, however, do anything to ease the rage Alexa felt as she watched the old phony pretend to hobble forward and pat each of the children on the head as they came forward to greet her.

Slowly, Camara approached her like a docile pet, her head down, slouching forward as a dog does after it has displeased its master. The she-wolf looked much smaller as she approached Violet than when she'd emerged from her cave to greet them the day before.

"How now, Camara?" Alexa heard the familiar wheezing in Violet's voice.

Camara bowed her head. "Mother," she said.

"What news?" Violet said, absently petting another boy's matted, filthy hair.

"Webb and Fawn have returned," she said, and she nodded toward the two boys.

Violet showed the gap in her teeth as she put on a simpering,

182

yet somehow malicious smile.

"Well done, young ones," she said, waving them forward. They walked toward her with their heads bowed. "How did you escape from the vicious hunters of Haventown?"

Fawn looked at Webb for guidance, but Webb was looking up into Violet's face. "We were helped by travelers to escape the jail and the city walls. They brought us back to Mother yesterday morning."

In an instant, Violet's simpering smile vanished and she stood tall, her head rising above the figures of the children. "Travelers? What travelers?" At her words, even Camara seemed to cower in fear. A few of the children closest to Violet backed away, but everyone was staring at her with rapt attention.

Violet stared at Camara, waiting for an answer, but it was Webb who spoke again.

"There was a girl named Alexa and her boyfriend Duster. They came from a farm to the south. They were nice, but Mother sent them away," he said. "The girl said that you kidnapped her brother, Grandmother. That's not true, is it?"

Violet did not answer Webb's question; instead she spoke to Camara. "Is this true? Did these travelers come to your den and you sent them away?"

Camara didn't answer. The great wolf trembled, unable to look up at the witch.

"You know your place. You know what it is you are to do," Violet said.

"Mother, they saved the lives of my children. I would not harm them," Camara said. Camara put her paws over her head, as if expecting her master's wrath.

"I have given you these lands to hunt. I have given you children to raise, and yet you betray me, Camara."

183

"No, Mother. I would never betray you," Camara said. A low whine escaped her as she flopped to the ground.

"Don't hurt her, Grandmother!" Webb screamed.

"You are right, young one," Violet said. "She will learn nothing if I punish her again."

Then Violet raised her arms, and from each hand a jet of golden fire exploded and hit Webb and another boy in the chest. They both crumpled where they stood. The witch turned her hands towards others, and suddenly another boy and Misha hit the ground with violent force.

Camara jumped forward in front of another of her sons, but just then, she was picked up by the force of Violet's power and thrust backwards toward the edge of the woods.

It was then that Alexa bolted toward the witch. Duster had been staring in shock, and didn't react until Alexa was already beyond the cover of the trees. Then he whispered harshly, "Alexa!" and darted after her.

Alexa ran forward into the clearing, straight at Violet, as another girl toppled from the force of the golden light. When Violet finally turned toward her, Alexa let out a strangled, wild scream of rage as she barreled toward the witch.

A jet of golden fire came at Alexa. She braced herself and then heard a sound like ringing metal. The spell seemed to bounce off of the air before Alexa and rebounded straight back at Violet, who ducked and scrambled back toward the mountain path faster than Alexa had ever seen her move.

Alexa ran right past the cave mouth after her, amidst the cries of Camara's children, while Duster struggled to catch up to her and was now screaming her name.

She had just begun a steep ascent when she caught sight of Violet ahead of her. They were in the shadows of the mountain when the witch turned to look at Alexa. Alexa saw the abject fear of age and desperation on Violet's face. Then Violet screamed a word that Alexa couldn't quite make out and vanished into thin air.

Alexa ran to the spot where Violet had vanished and looked frantically around, but she knew it was no good. She knew the witch had escaped. Once more Alexa let out a scream of rage and frustration, and then Duster was there. He put his arms around her and held her tightly as she thrashed and sobbed.

Alexa hated Violet with every fiber of her being, and for a brief crazed moment Alexa felt that it didn't matter whether her brother, her father, Duster, or even she herself lived or died. All Alexa knew was that she wanted to bring pain and death down on Violet. She had no other thought in her mind—no other feeling in her body. She tried to break free of Duster's grip again, but he wouldn't let go. Then, after several minutes of struggling and cursing, she was overcome with frustration and exhaustion and fell into Duster's arms.

It felt like hours later that she awoke, lying on a patch of rocky grass at the foot of the mountain, staring up at a sky of cloudless robin's egg blue and into Duster's panic-stricken face.

"Are you all right?" he breathed.

Alexa didn't move. She wasn't sure she could move just then. She didn't feel any pain, but it seemed that she had lost all awareness of her own body. She blinked and Duster's face seemed to relax a little above her.

"Hey," he said. He had taken her hand in his and was rubbing it gently. It took Alexa a moment to realize that she could feel the warmth of his fingers in her palm. She could feel him shaking as he pressed her hand to his chest.

Alexa breathed and smelled the scent of damp earth. She heard the wind push softly through the trees.

Alexa knew she was alive.

She rolled on to her side. "I'm sorry," she said.

"For what?" Duster said, holding out his hand as he stood.

Alexa took it and pulled herself to her feet. "I could have gotten us killed," she said.

As she looked down the path toward the mouth of the cave, she saw some of Camara's children huddled around a few bodies. Camara was walking gingerly around, her head low. There was a gurgling whine that Alexa thought might be the sound of the she-wolf crying.

Camara raised her head and let out a howl of grief. Alexa couldn't make the sound herself, but she understood it.

Alexa started back toward the cave, but Duster touched her arm. "I'm not sure we should go back there," he said.

"We have to."

They walked back into the small clearing near the cave. There were four bodies lying inert on the damp ground. A few children were scattered around each of them, talking quietly and shaking their heads.

Alexa went to where she saw Fawn kneeling in tears next to a body she couldn't see because it was blocked by Camara's enormous body. As she passed around the great wolf, Alexa saw Webb's tiny body on its back, his arm bent at an awkward angle, his legs splayed out. There was a trace of blood on his cheek, and his eyes were wide and vacant.

Alexa knelt down next to Fawn and reached out to touch Webb's face. He was still warm. She closed his eyes.

Alexa felt a shudder and realized that she was about to start sobbing again, but she took several deep breaths, concentrating on the face of the boy, until she mastered the impulse. She got to her feet and turned to face Camara.

"I am sorry for your children," Alexa said.

Camara whined and growled feebly. Her body shook as

she sat down on her great haunches.

Alexa reached out tentatively and patted the fur of the great wolf. At the touch, Camara raised her large head and looked down at Alexa, examining her face for several moments.

"Come and talk with me," the great wolf said.

Duster watched nervously as Alexa walked next to Camara. When the pair came to the mouth of the cave he made to follow, but Alexa glanced back at him and shook her head.

Camara went in first. The cave was dark, but the area near the entrance was lit by the bright sunlight outside. It was a large cavern with a smooth, stone floor. Alexa could see a small ring of stones for a fire, and many small stacks of straw that she assumed were the beds of Camara's children.

Camara came to the edge of the ring and stared down into the burnt timbers. "You are brave and powerful, Alexa Flynn. You saved my children once. You tried to save them again. If it were not for you, I have no doubt that Violet would have killed them all. I do not understand how you survived her killing spell. It didn't harm you at all. Your magic must be great."

"My magic is nothing. I don't even know how to control it," Alexa said.

"For many years I have served the crimson lady, and I have never before watched her flee before a foe. She ran from you in terror. Your power, even if you don't understand it, must be great. She fears it — and that old witch fears nothing," Camara said.

Alexa said nothing. She waited patiently for Camara to speak. Alexa knew that whatever she was going to say, Camara needed to say it on her own terms.

"I come from beyond the mountain range, far to the north. I am the daughter of the great wolf king, Amartus. For generations Amartus ruled over the wolves of the north, and brought to us peace and plenty. Then one day human hunters came, and there was a great battle and my father, my mother, and the rest of my pack were killed. I was just a pup and fled in terror. I walked the lands wearily, hunting where I could and avoiding human beings.

"Then one day I met Violet, and she recognized me as the last of the great wolves and offered me a deal. She gave me lands to hunt, and promised me what I desired most in the world — pups of my own to raise. When I was old enough, Violet brought them to me a few at a time. It didn't matter that the pups were human. I just wanted to feel the bond of the pack again. In return, I was to protect Violet's lands from intruders.

"I felt blessed. Violet had given me everything that I'd lost as a pup. Each time she visited was a celebration. The children came to know her as a grandmother. But in the last several months, she has become dangerous. When she was angry, she hurt me with her magic, but I didn't dare resist. I knew that if she wanted to, she could harm my children.

"She knew it, too. The last few times she has threatened to hurt my children, and she has shown me visions of their deaths. These have been the most painful punishments I'd received until today.

"I know now that she has enacted a very ingenious plan by giving me children. She had the perfect way to ensure my allegiance." Camara put her head down.

"She is cunning," Alexa said. "But you understand now why she must be destroyed. While she lives your children will never be safe."

Camara didn't raise her head. "I understand that now," she said.

"So please help me. Take us to her keep. We have to finish this," Alexa pleaded.

"The road is dangerous. And now the witch knows you are coming. It is very likely that we will fail to reach her keep," Camara said.

"You're probably right. But I have to try to save my family. You must understand that."

Camara walked slowly back to the mouth of the cave. She turned her enormous head toward Alexa, the pink scarred skin on the side of her face glowing eerily in the dim light.

"I will help you, Alexa Flynn."

CHAPTER 14
THE HAUNTED GROVE

A half hour later, Duster, Alexa, and Camara bid farewell to Camara's children and walked through the last few hundred yards of sunlight they would see for many days, and entered the woodlands at the foot of the mountains. The climb was not difficult, because here the ascent was gradual. The woodlands ended where the terrain became steeper and rockier a few miles ahead.

Once they were within the confines of the woods, they walked in silence and stayed close together. It was just as Alexa was staring up at the last rays of sunshine peering in through the high branches that Camara spoke to them. "You were wise to ask for my help in finding Violet's keep," she said. "I was not the only thing guarding it. It is magically protected from location unless Violet brought you or has invited you there before."

"We certainly weren't invited," Alexa said.

"I was brought there as a pup, and spent some years within the keep. Once you have been brought there or invited, she cannot hide her keep from you again," Camara said.

"Well, that's good, right?" Duster said.

"That depends," Camara said. "There is one more guardian we must all overcome. In a little time, we will come to the haunted grove. It is an area of the woodland where nothing grows. Its trees are spoiled and twisted. The grove is frozen in death. Violet commands the terrors within. If she has invited you, you will pass through it unharmed. Nevertheless, it is a terrible trek to undertake. It is like walking through the end of the world. However, if you enter without her permission, the evil of that grove will be set upon you."

At this point, Duster and Alexa both stopped. Alexa felt weakness in her limbs and leaned against a nearby tree to support herself. Duster stood near her, his face white and his brow glistening with sweat.

The wolf stopped and turned toward her terrified companions. "I have walked through the grove at the witch's invitation before. But even I do not know the terrors that await us when we enter the grove uninvited."

They walked what seemed only to be a few steps more, but it must have been several hours because the little sunlight that reached them through the high trees faded, and they could see only patches of hazy twilight when Camara said, "We are close."

Finally, they came to a place in the woods in which the darkness was more encompassing. Duster and Alexa could see just a few feet in front of themselves, but they kept walking steadily behind Camara. The wolf's padded steps seemed even lighter and quieter in the darkness.

They walked slowly through the thickening darkness, and Alexa was shocked when she walked into Camara, standing stiffly before two trees bent so that they created a natural archway. She pushed gently away from the hindquarters of

191

the enormous gray wolf. As she put her hands on Camara's back, she felt the great breathing cage of the beast take a rattling breath.

"We are here," Camara said.

Alexa looked into the darkness of the grove and could see nothing—no movement, no colored eyes flicking open and shut, no sign of movement. She listened intently and heard no sound.

As Duster came to stand next to her he crunched some leaves underfoot, and the sound was loud and intrusive into the quiet stillness of the wood.

Alexa put her hand in Duster's, and then pulled him forward to stand next to Camara. She put her other hand gently on the wolf's fur. "Let's try and stick together," she said. "Whatever's in there will have an easier time attacking us if we're separated."

"That is wise, human," Camara said.

Duster brought Alexa's hand to his lips and kissed the back of it gently. "I won't leave you," he said.

They walked beneath the bent boughs into the grove, and immediately a hazy light emanating from above them dazzled Alexa's eyes. It had appeared from the outside of the grove that there was a perfect darkness within, but it was actually easier to see within the grove than it had been outside of it.

Alexa decided that it must be part of the magic of the grove, but the thought did not cheer her. It was horrifying to look at the gnarled, moss-covered trunks. The branches and shadows seemed to take the forms of demons and beasts that looked ready to pounce on the intruders. Alexa wished that she couldn't see in here at all.

She looked up to see webs crossing the upper boughs of the trees, and although she couldn't see them properly, she saw the nebulous shapes of what must have been enormous spiders climbing from branch to branch. She couldn't make out their black eyes in the darkness, but there was a shiny reflection in the front of the bodies that Alexa could only guess was the unnatural light reflecting on their many eyes. At first she heard the ominous clicking sound and didn't recognize it, but then she realized it was the pincers of many spiders combining to create a terrifying, chitinous symphony.

Even the ground in the grove seemed to writhe beneath her feet, and at first she was afraid that she was standing on a bed of snakes. But they appeared to be nothing more than the tendrils of menacing vines that covered the ground and draped the tree trunks and boughs near them.

It was a long while until they moved. Even Camara stood still just beyond the entrance to the grove, and for a brief moment Alexa looked back to see if perhaps they could retreat and escape the terror. But the archway they had entered had disappeared from sight, and everything behind them was unyielding darkness.

Alexa breathed heavily and decided that there was nothing else to do, and took the first step into the grove.

Duster and Camara saw her move ahead and stepped forward to stay with her.

Alexa had expected at this first step that the forces of the grove, the sinister vines and trees, as well as the spiders overhead, would immediately spring to action and attack them. But it didn't happen. The vines beneath their feet slithered about, and the spiders seemed to follow them closely, but no attack came.

Alexa dared not hope, but she felt that maybe Camara's previous trips through the grove were enough to keep these monsters at bay. Perhaps they recognized her, and thought that since Violet allowed her to pass through before, all that passed with her now were also allowed to go unharmed.

This one fleeting hope gave her the courage to continue on in that horrible place.

It wasn't until they'd been walking for nearly twenty minutes that they came to anything that appeared immediately dangerous. They came to a place in the grove that they could not pass together. Here the trees were packed tightly, and the small path they had been following wound through them, but it was clear that they would have to pass through this area one at a time.

Alexa knew it was a trap—she was sure of it—but she didn't dare speak in the grove in case it aroused the attention of the terrifying creatures that surrounded them. Or worse yet, if it attracted the attention of terrors they had not yet seen.

They stopped before the small woodland pass and Alexa looked at both Duster and Camara. Alexa pointed to herself and then to the path. Then she pointed at Camara and then the path. Finally, she pointed to Duster and the path.

Camara nodded slowly, but Duster was shaking his head vigorously. He pointed to himself and then to the path, and then to Alexa.

But Alexa didn't let him finish. She plunged forward before Duster could finish his hand signals.

Alexa turned sideways to slide into the narrow gap between the trees, and knew immediately that something had happened. She was in a small clearing, with a single tree-stump in the center of it. The light was grayer here, but she could still see the entire clearing. There were no spiders in the trees above. The ground was soft, dewy grass. It was as if she'd stepped into another world.

She turned back to the gap between the trees and waited.

Any moment now Camara and Duster would emerge and they could continue. But after a few seconds, she knew something was wrong.

They weren't coming. Alexa went back to the gap between the trees and tried to slide between them again, but she found the gap was much too small this time. She peeked around the trees and could see nothing but darkness behind her.

Alexa felt tightness in her stomach and a burning sensation in her chest as she realized that she was completely alone. She had no idea where Duster or Camara were, or whether they were all right. All Alexa knew was that whatever she faced from this point forward, she faced alone.

She turned back to the clearing and noticed that a handsome man with a sneering face sat on the stump that had been empty just moments before. He was dressed in neat cerulean robes.

"Breg, what are you doing here?" Alexa said.

"You should never have come here," he said.

"I had no choice," Alexa said.

Breg laughed mirthlessly. "The little warrior girl...always taking on the responsibilities that no one else can," he said. Alexa noticed that his eyes glinted even in the gray haze of the grove.

"My family will be destroyed unless I stop her," Alexa said.

She took a step toward Breg. He shook his head and stood. He was almost a foot taller than she was, and he glared icily at her with his brilliant blue eyes. He stood a long time, staring at her, waiting for her to cower, to back away, but she didn't. She stood and waited until Breg spoke.

"Nothing can save your family now, you realize," he said quietly.

"That's not true—" Alexa began.

Breg cut her off. "Michael is dead. The crimson lady has

taken his power and his life. There will be no way for you to defeat her now that she has accomplished this," he said. "Your father will die when you fail to destroy her." Alexa began to shake her head, but Breg kept going. "Either she will destroy you or she will flee before you reach her keep. Either way, you will fail. You will not be able to fulfill your end of the bargain with my queen."

Alexa felt tears stinging her eyes as Breg spoke, and then the tightness in her stomach and the burning sensation she felt were gone. She felt total emptiness after hearing Breg's words. But there was just something different about Breg's manner. He seemed a little edgier, angrier than he had seemed the times she'd met him before. And his eyes...there was something about his eyes.

Although Breg was not pleasant normally, Alexa felt an acute oddity in the situation, and she stood there drinking it in through her pores, trying to maintain her focus on where she was and what she was doing.

"I've come to offer you a new deal," he said.

"What is it?" Alexa said.

"Your brother and father are lost. Those who were foolish enough to accompany you here are lost in this wood forever. I offer you one last chance to save someone you care about."

"Why?" Alexa said. "Why not just let me fail and let everyone die?"

Breg didn't respond. Alexa could tell that he had not expected this response. His brilliant blue eyes held her stare, but Alexa refused to look away.

"There is one you might still save," he said. "The one you desire most."

And Alexa knew what would happen before it did. She looked into the darkness beyond Breg and saw a figure emerge with a plodding, rhythmic gait. As the figure stepped into the gray of the clearing, Alexa saw the oval of her mother's face, expressionless in the gray light. Alexa remembered the last time she'd seen her mother's face, and heard Violet's wheezing laughter in her ears.

"You're not Breg," Alexa said. She nodded toward the other figure in the clearing. "And that's not my mother."

Suddenly, the gray light disappeared and Alexa was plunged into darkness. Then she heard a spitting hiss to her left. Alexa reacted instinctively, jumping back and ramming herself into the tightly grouped trees behind her.

She heard the shuffling sound of many legs padding across the ground, and knew that there were creatures all around her.

Without thinking, Alexa put her hands out and yelled, "Light!" From her hands came an iridescent glow that quickly spread through the small clearing. Alexa saw that there were giant spiders everywhere. The largest, with a body wider than a pig, was standing on the stump where Breg had been. Alexa looked to the spot where her mother had appeared, and there was a spider almost as large, frothing at its black mouth and clicking madly.

When the light appeared, the spiders, who had not seen light like this for many years, stared, their glassy, insect eyes drawn in by the stark power of the light. Alexa did not know how she had made the light appear, but she focused all her energy on keeping it glowing from her hands. The spiders were mesmerized by it, and although they hissed and sputtered, none of them moved toward it.

Alexa looked quickly around the clearing. She saw that the path continued on the other side of it, and knew that she would have to walk across the clearing to get to it. She began the slow trek, careful not to step on the legs of any of the spiders staring

197

up at the light. She held her breath as she came even with the great spider sitting on the stump and hissing at the light.

Once she was past him, she began to breath rapidly and felt panic rise up in her chest. The light wavered for a moment, and before she could think about it, Alexa dropped her hands and ran full out into the woods.

It took the spiders a few seconds to recover their wits after the disappearance of the light, but Alexa quickly heard the rapid pattering of their feet beating against the ground and the trees as they chased her into the forest.

She ran without knowing where she was going or where Duster or Camara were. She had one thought—to run as fast as she could from the spiders.

She ran for several minutes, a stitch tearing painfully into her side, until she unexpectedly burst into another clearing. Alexa slammed into the gigantic backside of Camara as the wolf reared up on her hind legs to claw at a spider that was attacking her.

Alexa fell back to the ground. She took a moment to gather her wits about her and look around. Alexa saw several spider bodies strewn around the clearing. Some had vicious bites and slashes in their bodies; some had their legs torn off.

It was clear that Camara was winning her battle against the spiders. Many of them were already backing away from the she-wolf. As she felled the biggest spider in the clearing, many of his comrades turned and fled. A few backed away slowly, but most ran off in fear of Camara's vicious claws and her razor-like teeth.

Alexa was still on the ground, panting, when the last spider scurried away. Alexa looked up at Camara and the wolf shook her head violently, still stamping the ground in her rage.

Alexa stood up and went to her. She was about to reach out

and touch her fur, but decided against it. "Camara, it's over. They're gone."

Camara twitched once, almost convulsively, and turned her head toward Alexa. There was a brief moment when the great wolf's eyes flashed that Alexa felt like she might attack.

"Camara! Camara!" Alexa said. She reached out tentatively and patted Camara's fur. The she-wolf was still growling menacingly, but didn't move. It took another few minutes before the growling ceased and Camara's breathing slowed.

"This place is a nightmare," Camara said.

Alexa nodded in agreement. "Have you seen Duster?"

"No, but if we continue I daresay we'll find him. Whether or not it is too late—"

"Come on!" Alexa said, and sprinted onto the path. Camara caught up to her easily and they darted through the woods. Alexa felt her clothes tear on passing branches, and felt many of them claw into her flesh as she ran through the forest, but she didn't care. All Alexa could think about was Duster trapped in a clearing being attacked by spiders.

Alexa and Camara came to another clearing and darted into it. Alexa stopped abruptly when she saw two people facing each other.

Duster stood with his back to them, trembling. Directly in front of him was his mother. She looked younger than Alexa had ever seen her. She was a small woman with dark features in a plain, canvas dress. Alexa saw that she had a long, smooth neck. The bridge of her nose set her eyes in the same pleasing shape as Duster's.

It took Alexa a moment to hear that she was speaking to him in a low, urgent voice. "I don't understand. You can bring me back," she said.

"I can't. I can't. I'm so sorry," he said. His voice was

unnaturally high. Alexa could hear the terror in his voice.

"You would betray me for that girl?" His mother said.

"No, Mother. I would never betray you, but I have to help her," he said miserably.

Suddenly, Alexa saw a vision of herself emerge from the other end of the clearing and walk slowly out to where Duster stood facing his mother. The face of the girl was a slightly altered version of her own. There wasn't a tangible difference, but there was a cold beauty to it that Alexa had never recognized in her own reflection. The vision wore a beautiful green satin gown. She walked slowly, her hands together as she came forward.

The real Alexa shook herself out of the shock that had first accompanied this strange vision and began to go out into the clearing.

Suddenly, Camara put her massive claw out and blocked her way. "Do not interfere," she said. "This is his test."

Alexa moved around to the side a little so that she could see better, and even catch a glimpse of Duster's face as he experienced the strange scene. Duster didn't notice the vision of Alexa until it was almost right behind his mother. Suddenly Alexa saw something glint in the vision's hands, and there was a flash of silver as she stuck a knife into the back of Duster's mother.

Duster's mother let out a gasp, but didn't have the breath to scream and fell to her knees.

Duster screamed, "No!" but stood rooted to the spot.

Then, the vision of Alexa jerked the knife out of the woman's back. As Alexa watched, Duster's mother seemed to deflate. Her features aged rapidly, and she was already covered in wrinkles and age spots that had not been there moments before. The vision of Alexa reached out and brought the blade across the old woman's neck and slit her throat. She fell forward onto the grass with a sickening thud.

Duster screamed and ran forward at the vision of Alexa. He grabbed her by the throat and began to strangle her. The vision of Alexa in the clearing fell to her knees, and her eyes began to roll into the back of her head.

And suddenly the spell lifted. Alexa saw Duster with his hands on the head of a giant spider. There were spiders all around him, closing in. Duster seemed to take no notice. He was still screaming and throttling the spider that he believed to be Alexa in the center of the clearing.

Alexa put her hands up to make the light again, but only a faint glow flickered for a moment and then went out.

It was Camara who leapt into the clearing and scattered the spiders that were closing in around Duster. Frothing at the mouth and clicking madly, they backed away from the great wolf as she slashed at them with her claws and lunged at them with her powerful jaws.

The spiders had become mortally afraid of Camara, and none dared come near her to attack Duster. As the wolf slashed and lunged, the spiders gave up their game and retreated into the darkness of the woods.

Meanwhile, Duster still struggled with the spider that had been where the vision of Alexa had been moments before. He throttled the spider and cried out, "No!" over and over again. Once the spider fell from his grasp and was too weak to scurry away, Duster pounded it with his fists as tears streamed down his face. Finally, the spider shuddered and moved no more.

Duster continued to punch the body. Alexa watched him in silence for a few moments, unsure what to do. Finally, Alexa moved slowly and tentatively around Duster. She said his name quietly, but he didn't seem to hear her. He continued to scream and pound the dead body of the spider.

Alexa finally came forward and stood near him. She was afraid to touch Duster, but he would not respond to her voice. Finally, she knelt next to him.

At once, he seemed to finally see the body of the spider before him and recoiled from it. Then he looked at Alexa, and there was a blazing fury in his eyes that Alexa had never seen before. His usually benevolent, handsome face was twisted into a look of grotesque anguish.

"How could you do that?" he screamed.

Alexa felt spittle on the side of her face and neck. "I didn't. It wasn't me," Alexa said feebly.

Duster didn't say anything. He was panting, the look of anguish still distorting his features.

Alexa reached forward and touched his shoulder, still on her knees in front of him. He recoiled and scrambled to his feet, his hands balled into fists of rage. Alexa was certain that it was only a matter of moments before he attacked her.

But then Camara came to stand next to Alexa and spoke. "What you saw wasn't real. That is the magic of this grove. It shows us visions to tempt us or drive us mad."

Duster remained silent. His breathing began to slow, but the fury in his eyes was still there. He stared at Alexa, who was still kneeling before him, unable to look him in the eye.

It was several minutes before Duster seemed to regain even a little of himself. The look of anguish did not vanish, but he finally was able to tear himself away from the spot and sit down by a tree. He put his head in his hands and sat for a long while.

Alexa didn't move either. She knelt wearily in the clearing. The entire journey through the forest and the haunted grove seemed to weigh her down, until she rolled onto her back and, breathing heavily, stared up at the trees in the gray light.

"We must go on," Camara said. She stalked slowly around

the clearing, inspecting the trees. The great wolf walked onto the path on the far side of the clearing and called back to them, "It's this way."

"No!" Alexa said, and flung her arm over her face.

Alexa felt strong hands lift her up and place her on her feet. She swayed slightly and the hands steadied her. She looked into Duster's face. It was stained with grime and tears, but the rage was gone.

Duster looked down and gently touched the half-moon bracelet on Alexa's wrist. She felt the gentle brush of his finger against her skin.

Duster's face was weary and sad. Alexa wanted nothing more than to reach up and touch his face, but she didn't. She couldn't shake the memory of his face while he attacked the vision of her. Alexa wasn't sure Duster would ever look at her the same way again. She looked away from him, and muttered, "I can't. I can't."

He came around to stand next to her, and she felt his hand close on hers.

"Come on," he said.

Together, they followed Camara out of the clearing into the woods.

Chapter 15
The Keep of the Crimson Lady

They walked silently along the woodland path. The only sounds Alexa heard were their footsteps and the great rattling breaths of the wolf.

Alexa held tightly to Duster's hand, but didn't look at him for several minutes. Finally, she glanced up. She saw his face was strained with worry.

"Are you all right? Are you hurt?" Alexa said.

Duster shook his head, but refused to look at her. "It's nothing. I'm fine," he said.

They began to climb in earnest. The gradual slope they had encountered coming out of the valley had become a steep and treacherous ascent into the mountains. Camara still walked lightly, leaping gracefully from rock to rock. The great wolf looked back often to see how well Duster and Alexa were keeping up.

Duster climbed quickly, but with great effort. He often grabbed a stone, tried his grip, decided that he didn't like it, and tried a different one. Alexa could tell he was able, but that he had little experience climbing.

However clumsy Duster might've looked, Alexa was lucky not to topple down the mountain on several occasions. She was the novice climbing through the unsteady maze of rocks and weed grasses. Alexa was very tentative, and had a great deal of difficulty pulling herself up through the slippery rocks.

It was twilight when they finally reached a plateau where they could look down onto another small valley, and then one final steep ascent into the next outcropping of rock, upon which stood a weathered stone turret with a heavy oak door: Violet's keep. The top of the turret was a spiral of stone that pierced the twilight like a blade.

Alexa came over to the edge of the plateau and looked down at the steep decline into the next valley. She stepped quickly back onto the flat ground of the plateau. "Should we try to climb down tonight or wait until morning?" she asked.

"It's too steep," Duster said. "We should wait. We should be able to reach the keep by sundown tomorrow."

Camara growled. She stood back from the edge and was still staring at Violet's keep. "Any delay will give the witch more time to perform her spell. I doubt we will be able to defeat her after she has taken your brother's power. The choice is yours," she said to Alexa.

Although it seemed like suicide to try and descend the mountain at night, Alexa thought they didn't have much choice. Camara was probably right—they had to get to Violet as quickly as possible.

"We're going to have to risk it," she said.

Duster frowned, but nodded as they began the treacherous descent.

In a few places they slid down, only grabbing on to shrubs or rolling into outcroppings, but they made their way quickly down the mountainside. Camara still traveled quickly and surely, but it was only a matter of luck that Alexa and Duster made it down unharmed. They reached the valley before the peak upon which stood Violet's modest keep.

They rested for about an hour in the valley, eating quickly and lying down on the grass, trying to find the strength and courage for the final leg of their journey. It was Camara who once again urged them on.

Luckily, the moonlight was bright and the stars shone with undiminished glory as they began their second slow ascent.

As they climbed, Alexa had the sinking feeling that something was terribly wrong. They encountered no guardians, and the slimy, difficult rocks they'd encountered when they entered the mountain range were not to be found on this peak. There was a roughly made, meandering path of dirt that led up the mountainside.

When Alexa voiced the concern that this path led too easily to Violet's keep, Duster shook his head, but didn't offer explanation.

It was Camara who explained why she believed that the way into Violet's keep seemed so easily accessible.

"She has already left great obstacles before this. Violet is arrogant, and probably believes that no unwanted guest could infiltrate those. Also, if Violet's keep is protected from magical entry, she would need a place near it to bring herself by magic and then approach it on foot. She would not want that way to be difficult. She is powerful, but using her magic taxes her and she has often returned here very weary," Camara said.

They followed the dirt path up the mountain. It was as sunlight broke in the east that they came through a small pass and emerged before Violet's keep. The weathered stone of the turret was cracked, and there was a dark moss spread about the walls.

The building itself was a perfect cylinder, and they circled it once to find that there was but one entrance, a heavy pair of oaken doors where the dirt path ended. There were no windows, but the upper half of the turret had arrow slits all the way around about five feet apart.

The spiral at the top of the turret looked less sinister in the morning light.

As Duster, Camara, and Alexa stood before the doors, Duster said aloud what they were all thinking. "How do we get in?"

"Will the doors open for you because you've been here before?" Alexa asked Camara.

The she-wolf strode forward and stood before the great doors—nothing happened. Camara spoke. "I wish to pass." Still nothing happened.

"Maybe we should try to climb it," Duster suggested.

"Even if we could get up there, we couldn't fit in those arrow slits. They're too narrow," Alexa said.

Duster nodded. Alexa came forward and stood directly before the door. She reached for one of the handles.

Duster screamed, "No!" but it was too late. Alexa touched the handle and felt a great jolt of electricity coursing through her body, but she refused to let go of the handle and began to force the current the other way. After a few moments, she could feel the crackling power under her fingertips gathering at the door.

Alexa felt a great calm as she pushed forward and felt the door splintering at the force of her touch. She grabbed the handle with her other hand as well and rushed forward, churning her feet on the grass, pushing the heavy door back.

Suddenly the doors exploded inward and Alexa was left in the doorway, still holding one of the wrought iron handles.

After the smoke cleared, Camara and Duster came up on either side of her. Camara was looking eagerly into the hall, but Duster was staring at Alexa, a mixture of shock and pride on his face.

He smirked a little at her — it was the first time since before he'd had the vision of her in the haunted grove that Alexa had seen him smile — and nodded. "Nice work," he said.

"So much for a surprise attack," Alexa said.

Then Camara leapt forward into the keep. Alexa and Duster followed her into a large stone hall that opened all the way to the spire on the top. There was a great spiral staircase that led all the way up to the next level, about seventy feet above them.

There was an eerie stillness in the vast hall. Alexa looked to the upper level but could see no movement or hear any sound. Suddenly, Camara leapt onto the first step and began bounding up the staircase before Alexa and Duster could move.

Then the staircase burst apart. It maintained its basic shape of a spiral, but the steps were thrust from each other by an unseen force and suspended in midair. Each step was at least three feet from the next. Camara had to stop abruptly, and struggled to keep all four paws on one step as she balanced about twenty feet from the floor.

Alexa ran forward and pushed on the first stair and leapt for the next one. She reached it easily and scrambled to her feet. Duster quickly followed. Camara made a mighty leap and landed delicately on the stair above her. The great wolf began a rhythmic leaping and landing, and steadily climbed the steps.

The going was once again much slower for Duster and Alexa. The first few steps were no problem, but as they climbed higher, fatigue set in and it became harder and harder for them to make the jumps to the next stair. About halfway, Duster and Alexa sat side-by-side on a step and, panting heavily, tried to figure out how they would reach the top.

208

"What are we going to do? If we keep this up one of us is likely to fall," Duster said.

"I think that's the idea," Alexa said.

They looked up and saw that Camara was moving a little more slowly than she had at the beginning, but she was very near the top of the staircase. Duster stood up and reached out to help Alexa up.

"We have to keep going," he said. He swung his arms forward and sprung forward toward the next step.

Then suddenly, the staircase reassembled. Duster almost missed his step but managed to get hold of it with one hand. Alexa ran up and grabbed the hand and frantically pulled him up. As she struggled with Duster's weight, she saw out of the corner of her eye a dark shape fall past the staircase, and heard a sickening thud.

Once Duster was back on to the stair, Alexa leaned over and looked down. She saw Camara lying in a heap on the stone floor, a pool of blood forming underneath her broken body.

Alexa ran down the steps recklessly. She wasn't worried about the stairs moving under her. All Alexa knew was that she had to get to Camara.

Alexa reached her quickly and knelt down next to the great wolf. Her great rattling breaths were shallow now. Her piercing eyes were glassy and unfocused. Her hind legs were splayed out awkwardly beneath her. Alexa knew Camara could no longer feel them.

"Camara! Camara!" Alexa said.

The she-wolf's voice was no more than a low growl. "I'm dying. You must destroy her."

Alexa shook her head fiercely. "We can't do it without you," she said.

"You must...or she will continue to destroy...families...

like yours and mine," she said. The wolf's chest heaved as she coughed heavily. For one moment, the glassy eyes of the she-wolf found Alexa's, and they looked confused, frightened — and then the fire went out of them. Camara moved no more.

Violet's wheezing voice echoed through the tower. "Through sheer luck and the guidance of the dog have you reached my keep. Now you have nothing more to protect you, Alexa Flynn. Michael's power will be mine."

"Come down here and fight!" Alexa screamed up into the tower.

Violet's voice echoed again. "There is no time for that. Why don't you come up?"

Then Alexa felt her body yanked up as if there was a rope around her waist, and she rose quickly through the air along the staircase. She struggled against the power dragging her up and spun wildly, crashing into the staircase. She felt the stone against her head and reached up to find a hot wetness on the side of her face, then pulled her hand back dizzily and saw the stain of crimson on her palm as she ascended into the upper level of Violet's tower.

When Alexa reached the top, she dropped onto a rough stone floor. Alexa lay there, panting and trying to keep from blacking out.

She heard another thump and heard Duster grunt as he was placed beside her. Suddenly, strong hands grabbed Alexa's wrists and bound them together. It wasn't until the person was tying her feet that Alexa thought to look at her captor. His pale features were grim. His jaw was set in anguish, and Alexa saw a wide gash on the side of his face, shockingly red against his pale cheek.

It was Michael.

"Michael, help me! We're here to rescue you," Alexa said.

210

But Michael made no indication that he had heard her. He quickly bound Duster's hands and feet and began to drag him away.

Alexa looked over at Duster and saw that his eyes were closed — he was unconscious.

Alexa was fighting to stay conscious herself, but still struggled vainly to break her bonds. All she managed to do was get the cords dug so deeply into her wrists that she started to bleed.

Michael dragged Duster around a corner and out of sight.

Alexa rolled over on to her hands and knees and tried several times to stand, which was very difficult with her hands and feet bound. But she accomplished it just as Michael came back around the corner.

"What are you doing?" she said, but as she looked at Michael, she realized that he couldn't hear her. His eyes were vacant and his movements were not the slouching, rushed movements she was used to her from her brother. He moved stiffly and methodically.

Michael pushed Alexa hard in the chest and she fell over again, hitting her back and head against the stone floor. Alexa saw black spots before her eyes as Michael began to drag her by her feet.

It was several minutes later that Alexa realized that she was no longer moving. She picked her head up and scanned around the room into which Michael had dragged her. It looked like a jail cell, with stone walls and a stone floor, and nothing in it except for a heavy iron bed in the center.

She glanced around and saw that Duster was not there. Michael was standing next to the bed, staring forward without expression.

"Michael! Michael!" Alexa hissed, but he made no indication

that he heard her.

At the sound of the door scraping across the stone, Michael turned and Alexa rolled over to see Violet stomp into the room. The old witch looked even more haggard than usual. She was carrying a small wooden bowl in one hand and a basket in the other. She placed the basket on the edge of the bed and put the bowl beside it.

"Get in," she hissed.

Michael obeyed. He climbed into the bed and lay stiffly on top of the mattress. He stared up at the ceiling.

"Michael!" Alexa screamed.

Violet laughed her wheezing laugh. "He can't hear you, my dear. He is under my spell."

The witch turned back to Michael and began fastening the leather bands that hung from the bedframe over his body. She fastened the first one over his shoulders, the next around his waist, and the last one at his ankles.

Alexa struggled to free her wrists from the cord around them. She looked around frantically to see if there was anything sharp she might use to cut them. Alexa knew she had only moments before it was done.

Once Alexa realized there was nothing near her, she said quickly, "Why bind him if he's under your spell?" Alexa really didn't care what Violet's answer might be. All she wanted to do was stall the witch so that she might figure out a way to escape.

"I will have to free him from my control before I take his power," she said simply, without turning to look at Alexa.

Out of the basket, Violet took a small wooden bowl, some dry gray feathers, and a slender bone. Then she reached in with both hands and removed a book and placed it next to Michael. She leafed through it unhurriedly until she found the page she wanted. This time she turned to look at Alexa wriggling on the floor. "Once I take his power, I will destroy you with it. It won't be long now," she said.

Violet turned back to Michael and began the sonorous incantation. Michael's eyes suddenly came into focus and he turned his head, looking at Violet and then quickly down at Alexa. He began to struggle against his bonds, but all he managed to do was shake the bed.

"No!" he screamed into the old woman's face as she leaned over him.

Alexa saw Violet reach down and pull Michael's shirt apart. Then the witch put her fingers into the bowl and when she removed them, Alexa saw blood on them. Violet smeared the blood across her brother's bare chest, his wrists, and his forehead.

Both Michael and Alexa were mesmerized by Violet as she continued the spell, until suddenly Michael went stiff and cried out.

Violet gasped and staggered a little, but continued the spell. Her speech became slurred. It was obvious that Violet was experiencing intense pain as her shoulders slumped forward.

Alexa thought wildly that the effort of the spell might kill the witch, but it didn't. Violet droned on.

Then Violet reached a shaking hand forward and touched Michael's forehead. Michael stiffened and let out a scream of rage, pain, and anguish like nothing that Alexa had ever heard before.

Without thinking, Alexa brought her knees to her chest and rolled to her feet and fell forward into Violet. As her head collided with the shrunken body of the old woman, Alexa felt a burning pain that started at the spot that was touching Violet and coursed through her entire body in seconds.

Alexa cried out, and then there was an explosion of intense

heat and Alexa was blown backward, smashing hard against the wall. Violet was blown in the other direction and slammed to the floor; the bed on which Michael was bound flipped over.

The last thing Alexa saw was the shrunken body of the witch crumpled on the stone, and as she began to lose consciousness Alexa had one thought: *I hope she's dead.*

***

Alexa woke to the sound of a heavy scraping and opened her eyes. She was still lying against the wall where she'd fallen, but as she moved her legs, she realized she was no longer bound.

Dizzily, she got to her feet and looked around. The bed was back on its legs in the center of the room, and Michael was huddled over it. As her brother backed up, Alexa saw Violet's shrunken shape strapped into the bed. She was looking frantically around, her eyes darting from Michael to the walls, and then finally at Alexa.

"Don't let him do it," she said.

Alexa came forward. "Do what?"

Michael came up next to her. He placed the spell book next to Violet and began to line up other items. He put the wooden bowl next to the book, and the bone and feathers next to that.

"I'm going to do to her what she planned to do to me. I'm going to take her power," Michael said without looking up.

"Michael, you can't do that," Alexa said. She reached out to touch him, but stopped herself. She stared at his profile. The blood was still on his forehead. His haughty features were almost unrecognizable as those of the sullen brother she had outshined for so many years.

He pretended not to hear her and continued to set up the components he needed for the spell.

"You'll be a monster like her —" Alexa began.

214

Michael cut her off. "Duster is in grave danger," he said. "If you are to save him, you must go to him now in the last room in this corridor. If not, he'll surely die. So you must decide, Alexa." He turned to her. "I'm giving you this one chance, Alexa. I will have her power no matter what. The question is whether or not you will forfeit Duster's life to try and stop me."

Alexa looked up into his face, but she couldn't see her brother any more. His face was twisted by greed and anger. Michael's boyish, sullen face looked as though an artist had altered it with a few brushstrokes, painting it into an unrecognizable sneer of conceit.

Alexa sighed and turned away.

She ran out of the room and down the hall. She stopped at the last doorway and looked in.

The room was another featureless cell. There was no bed in this one, but a great table was bolted to the floor. Duster, who was unconscious, was tied to the table with heavy leather straps.

At first, Alexa thought that Michael had lied and that Duster only needed to be untied. Then she saw the small smoldering flame on a rope that was tied to one of the table legs. Alexa's eyes followed the rope up to the ceiling, where she saw that it led to heavy chandelier, filled with burning candles, suspended by a single ring in the ceiling. She realized that as soon as the rope burned through, the chandelier would come crashing down on Duster.

First Alexa ran to the rope and tried to put out the flame by smothering it with her sleeve. The rope creaked and a strand snapped. When she pulled her hands away, the fire continued to burn. She realized that Michael's fire was magical, and that she wouldn't be able to put it out in time.

Then as Alexa lunged over the table she smelled the heavy

215

odor of oil, and realized that Duster and the entire table were covered in it. She grabbed for the strap that held his shoulders. Alexa fumbled it because her hands were shaking. She glanced up at the chandelier nervously.

Finally, she got the first strap off his shoulders and began to loosen the strap around his waist. She had just gotten it off when she heard a crackling sound. She didn't bother trying to unfasten the last strap. Alexa put her arms around Duster's body and heaved his weight toward her. She could only hope that his feet would slip out as she pulled.

At the first pull, she felt the strap catch and hold him halfway off the table. She rushed back up and pulled again. This time, Duster and Alexa fell to the floor just as the heavy iron chandelier crashed onto the table. In seconds, the table was consumed in fire.

Alexa scrambled to her feet and dragged Duster away from the flames. She pulled him by his arms into the hallway and shut the door behind her. She hoped that the fire would put itself out once it reached the stone floor.

Duster lay motionless. Alexa knelt next to him and was relieved to hear him breathing softly. She began slapping him softly on the cheek. She said his name over and over again. It was just as he opened his eyes that Alexa heard a wheezing scream of pain from down the hall.

As Duster stared up into her face, confused, Alexa shuddered. She knew it was done.

After a few seconds, Duster was able to push himself up on his elbows, and Alexa said, "Stay here."

She got up and walked slowly back to the room on the other end of the corridor. As she walked in, Michael stood in the center of the room, a maniacal look of triumph on his face. Alexa walked past him and stared down at Violet's body. It was shrunken and frail. The body looked as if it might turn to dust at any moment. Alexa looked into the witch's face, and it seemed like a formless mass of wrinkled skin and veins. It hardly resembled a human face.

Alexa sighed and closed her eyes. When she had thought about this moment before, she always imagined she would have a feeling of triumph and relief to know that this vile, power-hungry creature could no longer hurt Alexa or her family — but there was nothing.

Alexa was numb.

She took one more glance at Michael, who still stood triumphantly in the center of the room, and walked out.

She went back to where Duster still sat on the floor, looking up at her. His brow was creased in a look of concern as Alexa came back and knelt in front of him.

"Are you okay?" she said.

He nodded. He stared earnestly into her face. "Is Violet destroyed?" he asked.

Alexa nodded.

"So it's finally over?" he said.

Alexa shook her head sadly. She spoke quietly, almost to herself rather than to Duster. "No," she said. "It's only just begun."

CHAPTER 16
LOST AND FOUND

Alexa helped Duster to his feet. He stood with a grunt and asked, "What happened?"

Alexa looked at Duster for a moment and tears filled her eyes. She couldn't bring herself to tell him. She looked away and said, "Come on."

Alexa led Duster down the stairs. He walked gingerly, grimacing with pain as he stepped on his left foot.

"What's the matter?" Alexa said.

"My leg. I feel as though someone tried to tear it off," he said.

"That was me," Alexa said.

Duster looked at her in surprise, and then she explained about how she had found Duster strapped to the table, and how she'd struggled to pull him out of the straps at his ankles before the chandelier came crashing down.

"Well, I guess I should thank you for trying to tear my leg off," he said lightly.

Alexa smiled and shook her head.

When they reached the bottom of the stairs, they stopped

in front of Camara's body. The great wolf still lay next to the staircase.

"We should bury her," Duster said.

Alexa nodded.

They headed out the great oaken doors into the bright sunlight. The scent of the grass and the damp earth seemed to lift Alexa's spirits a little. She raised her face toward the sun and closed her eyes. She let its warmth caress her cheeks. She felt Duster beside her.

"It's beautiful, isn't it?" he said.

Without opening her eyes, Alexa said, "Yes."

Duster walked slowly over to a large rock and sat down. He held up his leg and began to make small circles with his foot. Then he rubbed the ankle. He stood up again and said, "Good as new."

Alexa had lowered her face from the sun, but hadn't moved. She opened her eyes and watched Duster test out his leg, but she wasn't thinking about him. Her thoughts were far away. They were in the little cottage on the outskirts of the Eckerly farm.

"Do you think my father is okay? Do you think the council kept up their end of the bargain?" she said.

Duster nodded slowly. "I don't know," he said. "All we can do is hope."

He walked past her and back into Violet's keep. He emerged a few minutes later with a shovel. Duster picked a spot that seemed level and pierced the ground. He began to dig in earnest.

Alexa watched him for a few moments and then looked back up at Violet's keep. Michael had still not come down.

The ground was soft and Duster made good progress fairly quickly. Alexa took over for him, and then they worked in shifts for the better part of a couple of hours until they'd made a hole large enough for Camara's body.

Duster had just climbed out of the hole when Michael finally emerged from the keep. He carried a large leather bag. The bag was so full of books and papers that it wouldn't close. As he approached them, Michael laid the bag on the ground.

"What are you doing?" he said.

"We're digging a grave for Camara," Duster said.

"That dog in the hall?" he said.

"She wasn't a dog. She was the queen of her race, and without her, we would never have gotten here," Duster said.

Michael looked back at the large heap in the hall. "Allow me," he said.

Michael put his arms out and Camara's body was slowly lifted from the ground, and glided effortlessly through the air until it hovered just over the hole that Alexa and Duster had made. Michael lowered his hands and the body lowered into the grave.

Duster made to begin refilling the hole with the great pile of earth they'd created next to it, but before he could get near it, Michael moved his hands and the pile collapsed and filled the hole on top of Camara's body.

"Thanks," Duster said.

Michael turned and nodded coolly toward Duster.

Alexa finally spoke. "We need to talk."

Michael nodded and walked over to the rock that Duster had sat on before.

"I'll go scout out the area and see if the way back is clear," Duster said, clearly trying to leave the Flynns with some privacy.

"No, Duster. Please stay," Alexa said as she sat on the ground in front of Michael. "I have no secrets from you."

220

Duster felt the color rise in his cheeks, but he didn't look at either Michael or Alexa. He hesitated for a moment, and then went to sit down next to her.

Alexa was looking up into Michael's haughty face while he sat on the rock, his head and shoulders well above theirs. He looked like a schoolmaster teaching his pupils.

"What happened?" Alexa said.

Michael frowned. "What do you mean?" he said.

"That night? After you left the clearing?" Alexa said.

Michael nodded grimly. "I knew then that I'd made a mistake. Violet's power was incredible. I couldn't do anything to free myself from it. No spells would work. I couldn't move. It was terrible. We were probably a half a mile away before I realized that the only power I still had was keeping you immobile. So in a rush of hope that you might be able to catch up to us, I released you."

"I stayed with Father. You almost killed him," she said.

Michael sneered at her. "I know that. I'm sorry about it now," he said.

Alexa, however, had a feeling that whatever he might say, Michael was not particularly sorry about any of his actions any more. "Then what?" Alexa said.

"Violet brought me here. She kept me under her spell for a long time, but there came a time when she tied me up on that bed and released me from the spell. Naturally I tried to fight my way out, but I could do no magic with my hands bound like that—no matter how angry I was. But she needed to release me. She began reading to me."

"What?" Duster and Alexa said together.

"That's right. She read to me from her spell book and began showing me spells. I asked her why she would bother teaching me more magic, and she said simply that the more knowledge

221

and power I had, the greater her gain would be when she took my power.

"I was torn. I wanted to learn, but I also wanted to break free and destroy her. I had a choice. So I vowed to stay her prisoner and not to try and destroy her as long as she continued to teach me magic. I figured that sooner or later a chance to escape would come along. She agreed happily.

"In the last couple of days she has allowed me to remain out of her control, and allowed me to read her spell book myself while I was bound to the bed. She sat with me and turned the pages herself, to make sure that I didn't attempt to break free.

"Then yesterday she came in to my room in great agitation and put me under her spell once more. I imagine that is when you arrived," he said.

Alexa nodded.

"The next time I awoke you were there. I knew what she was doing. I'd read that spell before. I was helpless," Michael said. For one brief moment, Alexa thought his face resembled its old sulkiness. "But you stopped her," Michael said.

Alexa nodded again. Michael stared at her icily, but Alexa held his gaze.

Duster looked from one to the other, but said nothing.

Michael looked down and then went on. "Then I awoke to find the bed on top of me, and you and Violet unconscious on the floor. Whatever happened, I found my arms free and I was able to get myself out of the bed and to put it upright using my magic. I quickly put Violet in the bed and strapped her in."

"But I don't understand," Alexa said. "What about Duster? How did he get in that room underneath the chandelier?"

"Violet must have forced me to tie him down while I was under her spell. I don't remember what I've done while she was in control of me," he said.

"But when I went to stop you from taking Violet's power, you told me he was in great danger. If Violet had lit that rope on fire, it would have crashed much earlier. Duster would already have been dead."

Michael smirked. "Figured it out yet?" he said.

Duster looked from Michael to Alexa and saw her eyes narrow in anger. "You did it," she said.

Michael nodded. "Yes. I knew you would try to stop me. And who knows? You might have. I don't understand your power, Alexa, but it must be very great to have saved you from me when I tried to attack you in our kitchen. It disrupted Violet's spell. It looked like you almost blew that room apart," he said, a little enviously.

"When I freed myself, I knew I had to guarantee that you wouldn't interfere," he said. "So I went down the hall and saw Duster chained up, and set Violet's machine of execution in motion. I imagine that her idea was for you to watch her take my power, and then to drag you down to watch Duster be crushed and burned to death. She enjoyed causing suffering," he said.

"Why didn't you just kill me so that I couldn't stop you? That would've been easier," Alexa said through gritted teeth.

"Completely unnecessary," Michael said, waving his hand. "I didn't want to kill you. After all, you had just saved my life." He stood up and looked down at his sister. There was an authoritative malice in the next words he spoke. "Besides, now we're even. You gave me my life. I gave you Duster's."

Alexa looked up at him with a mixture of revulsion and awe on her face. "You are a monster," she said.

Michael laughed again—a high, hysterical, mirthless laugh that echoed through the mountains around them.

Alexa stood up quickly and pulled Duster's shoulder.

"Come on, let's go," she said.

Duster hesitated. "What will you do now?" he asked Michael.

"I still have much to do...much to learn," he said. "I'm off to find other sorcerers."

"There are more?" Duster said, still looking up at him like an awed pupil.

Alexa was standing, her arms folded, waiting for Duster. She was trying to pretend that she wasn't the least bit interested in anything he had to say, but as Michael answered Duster's question, he looked directly at his sister. "Oh yes," he said.

"How do you know?" Alexa had spoken before she could stop herself.

Michael pointed at the bag he'd left on the ground. "Violet's journals speak of many sorcerers, some even more powerful than her," he said.

"So you're off to seek power?" Duster said.

Michael answered instantly. "Yes."

"Come on, Duster. Let's go," Alexa said, and turned to go.

Duster bounded up and ran after her. They were almost to the edge of the wood when they heard a great rumbling of stone. They looked back to see Michael, his arms raised high above his head. There was a faint glow of orange surrounding his entire body. Duster and Alexa felt a blast of cold air like winter had suddenly attacked them, and they heard Michael say loudly, "Ezair!"

Suddenly, the stones at the top of Violet's keep began to fall to the earth. Michael turned and walked away, but Alexa and Duster couldn't move. They were held mesmerized by the sight of the tower collapsing on itself, and watched as level after level of stones tumbled down, until the dust and the noise became unbearable and they had to retreat into the cover of the forest so that they could breathe freely once again.

Right as she was about to enter the woods, Alexa glanced back and saw Michael, carrying the heavy leather bag full of Violet's books, disappear into the edge of the forest on the other side. Then the dust became as heavy as blizzard snow and all was lost from sight.

Duster and Alexa traveled wearily through the mountains. They were exhausted and stopped immediately at nightfall, and slept straight through until morning on the plateau before descending again into the haunted grove.

The next morning, Duster seemed hesitant to go on, but Alexa wanted to start. The farther she got from the ruin of Violet's keep, the better.

"I don't think it'll be haunted any more," she said to Duster.

"Why not?" he asked.

"I believe that was part of her defense, but now that Violet's gone, the spell will have broken."

"What about the spiders?" Duster said.

"I don't know."

As they entered the grove it was dark, but not the unnatural dark that had seemed to envelope it on their first journey through it. And although Duster jumped at any rustling of leaves, thinking it was the scuffling of many padded feet, they met no spiders and passed through the grove without any trouble.

They passed through each of the clearings that they had been trapped and tempted in. Each one was totally empty and looked like a welcome place to stop, rather than a den of insanity, as they passed through this time.

It was as they passed the last of these that Duster spoke for the first time in many hours. "What did you see in yours?"

"I was tempted to leave you and Camara and to bring back

my mother," she said.

"And you chose not to?" Duster said. He stared at her in surprise.

"I knew it was a trick. I could feel it," she said. "Besides, I couldn't betray you," she said.

Duster looked down, and Alexa could tell that he was thinking about what he'd seen in the grove — the vision of Alexa killing his mother.

"You know I would never do anything like that," she said, putting her hand on Duster's shoulder. "If your mother were here I'd treat her kindly — like my own — "

Duster interrupted her. "It's not that. I knew you could never do anything like that. Even though I saw it, I knew in my heart it wasn't real. It was...."

"It was what, Duster?" Alexa asked.

"Guilt," he said.

He paused to gather himself, trying to figure out how to explain. He couldn't bring himself to look into Alexa's face. He held her wrist and his eyes were fixed on the half-moon bracelet as he finally spoke. "That vision of my mother asked me to abandon you — for her — and I wouldn't do it. It was like admitting to myself that you'd replaced her. Then when that ghost or whatever it was slit her throat, I went crazy. Not at you — at myself. I didn't know what I was doing. I was so — "

Alexa reached out and pulled Duster into an embrace. "It's okay. I understand. Remember what Camara said. This place is meant to test you and drive you mad. Its magic was powerful," she said. Duster trembled.

They stood together in silence for many minutes before they continued their journey back through the grove and into the forest near Camara's den. It was a long time after, when they were just emerging out of the woods and saw the cave entrance in the distance, that Duster spoke again. "What do you think Camara saw in the grove?"

"I imagine that she saw her children being threatened or killed. But that's why the magic didn't work on her. She'd already experienced that pain. She knew it wasn't real because it couldn't compare with the pain she actually felt," Alexa said.

Duster shook his head and they walked on toward Camara's den. When they were just a few yards away, they heard the shuffling of feet and froze.

The tall boy with the patchy beard emerged from the cave. He held his hand up to block the sun and blinked furiously, trying to see who approached. At last, he seemed to recognize Duster and Alexa. His shoulders slumped forward. He looked as if he might collapse.

"I have terrible news," Alexa said.

"Mother is dead," the boy replied.

"Yes, but how do you know?" Alexa said.

"Grandmother would never let her live. I knew when she left that she would never return to us. But it's better this way," he said, and sat down on the ground sulkily.

Duster came forward and knelt down in front of the boy. "What do you mean? Why is this better?"

But the boy didn't answer. He asked a question of his own. "The witch is dead?"

"Yes," Duster said.

"Tell us how you know that," Alexa said, more forcefully than she'd meant to.

The boy seemed to take no notice of her tone. "Because we remembered," he said.

"Remembered what?" Alexa said.

"Our families. Grandmother must have taken all of us from our families, and then used her magic to make us forget them.

Suddenly, yesterday, we were sitting in the cave, and it was like everyone woke up. We all remembered the families we had before Violet took us from our homes and brought us to Camara."

"So what happened?" Duster asked.

"They left. All of them. They all ran off to find their families. I don't imagine many of them will find them. Many of them came from very far away. The only ones who stayed were Fawn and me," he said.

"Where's Fawn now?" Alexa asked.

"Asleep in the cave," the boy said.

"Why did you stay? Don't you want to return to your family?" Alexa asked.

"Yesterday I remembered them. My brother, all three of my sisters. Mom and Dad. The witch killed them all. I have no one. Where would I go?" he said as tears welled up in his eyes.

"What about Fawn?" Alexa asked.

"He remembers his mother. Grandmother didn't hurt her when she took him from his home. Fawn decided not to go back yet. He wanted to wait until Camara returned. I believe he and I are the only ones who truly cared about her. Now that we know, I will go with him and help him find his family."

Duster and Alexa wanted to wait until Fawn woke up to tell him the news, but Camara's oldest son, whose name was Flint, refused. He told them that their reappearance without Camara would only anger and confuse Fawn, and that he would ask a lot of questions that they wouldn't want to answer.

Alexa begged him to reconsider.

Flint said, "It doesn't matter anyway. That's the way of the wolf—leave the dead and go on."

Alexa and Duster had a little food left in their packs, which they gave to Flint, and Duster even gathered more berries for the boys. Flint thanked them, and told them to leave quickly before Fawn woke up. Alexa wasn't sure it was the right thing to do, but Flint assured her that it was. "Don't worry about Fawn. I'll bring him back to his pack," he said.

With that Duster and Alexa left Camara's den, and continued their journey back through the valley of the wolf.

They made a wide arc around the walls of Haventown. Alexa and Duster were certain that helping Webb and Fawn escape would earn them either a death sentence or a long spell in the shabby jailhouse if they were to show their faces there again.

They made camp at nightfall once more. Late the next morning Duster and Alexa came to the woods on the far northern edges of Mr. Eckerly's land.

They quickened their pace, even though they were exhausted from the journey, with the end so close in sight. It was blazing noon when Alexa and Duster suddenly came out of the woods and found the path that led down through Mr. Eckerly's land. They ran past Duster's house without a glance and headed straight to Alexa's.

As the cabin came into view, Alexa stopped, overcome with emotion at seeing her home again. The timbers were still blackened from the fire that Michael had caused on the west side of the house.

She ran forward with tears streaming down her face. Duster jogged, easily keeping up with her. They turned up the steps onto the porch and Alexa stopped as she heard voices from inside.

She opened the door slowly and saw her father sitting at the kitchen table, a steaming mug before him. He looked thin and pale, but his elbows rested comfortably on the table and he laughed at the man sitting across from him.

As Alexa came in she ran to him without noticing anyone else in the room.

Just as she came to him, John Flynn turned and saw his daughter. His face lit up in joy and he rose gingerly to embrace her.

Alexa hugged her father and cried for a long time. She felt the beating of his heart against hers, and felt him clutching her with the same strength and desperate longing that she felt, and for that moment, she was blindingly happy.

At that moment, there were no other people in the world. Alexa and her father stood alone rejoicing at each other's return — hers from the dangerous journey to destroy the witch, and his from the clutches of death itself.

After several minutes of silence, Alexa heard the gruff voice of a man clear his throat. Finally she opened her eyes and broke slowly apart from her father.

She stopped to look around at the other people in the cabin. She found the man with the gruff voice first, seated directly across from where her father had been sitting. Alexa recognized the huge form and the grizzled scar across his face. It was Caelan. He stared at her warily, but gave her the slightest nod as their eyes met.

Alexa turned to see Donan leaning against the wall. Her muscular arms were crossed before her, and she was smiling happily at Alexa. Alexa couldn't help but think about the beautiful weather they'd had since Violet had been destroyed.

She turned to look at the other seat directly next to her father's, and saw the little man, Hack, wiping his nose. He seemed to take no notice of the joyful reunion.

Alexa looked back at the door and saw Breg, still neatly arrayed in his cerulean robes, looking distractedly out the window. Alexa immediately felt a lurch in her stomach at the sight of him, because the last time she'd seen him, or at least a vision of him, had been in Violet's grove. This Breg didn't resemble the terrible negotiator she had met there. If anything, Breg looked embarrassed—as if he was trying not to look at Alexa.

Then, emerging from the shadows near John's bedroom, came the little girl. Her face was shining with happy tears, and a light of the most comforting gold seemed to radiate from her skin.

It was the Queen of Calamity who spoke to Alexa. "You have done well," she said.

"Thank you," Alexa said, still clutching her father.

"As I told you, your power overcame the crimson lady," she said.

"But I just reacted. I didn't use my magic on purpose. I just tried to save my brother," Alexa said.

"We must talk," said the queen.

She came forward and held out her hand. Alexa took it and they walked outside. Alexa felt peaceful in the presence of the little girl.

"You do not understand the nature of your power," the queen said.

"No. I guess I don't," Alexa said.

"Other sorcerers—Michael, Violet, many others—have power that arises from their anger, hate, greed, jealousy. They can learn to control it through the use of spells, but their magic will eventually destroy them—as they all realize in the end. But your power is different. Your magic comes to you not when you're angry or when you want something, but when you would try to protect yourself and others. In short, your power comes from an infinite hope that all can be saved."

"I don't understand," Alexa said.

"Even should you learn the spells that other sorcerers know, you will find your magic works differently than theirs," the queen said.

"How?" Alexa asked.

"Since you are not letting hate, greed, or anger consume you like other sorcerers do, you will not suffer the same weakness and pain from using your magic," she said.

Alexa nodded, thinking about when Michael had collapsed after killing the robbers in the forest outside of Coyne.

"Sorcerers like Violet and Michael cannot understand magic like yours," the queen continued, "They seek to isolate themselves and hoard their power, taking it forcefully from others. Your power, on the other hand, grows naturally. Your magic is an extension of your selflessness, and it grows, as does your capacity to love." The queen lifted Alexa's hand and nodded at the bracelet on her wrist.

Alexa felt color rush into her cheeks as she looked away. But there was something that was still bothering Alexa. "Michael?" was all she could manage to say.

The little girl's face turned down in dimpled gloom. She said simply, "He has chosen his path."

"Did you know that Michael would leave? Is that why you made the bargain to bring back my father?" Alexa said.

"I can't see the future, but I could feel Michael's anger and lust for power," the queen said. "I thought that even if you succeeded in saving his life, he would be lost to you."

They stood in silence.

"Dad's going to be crushed. I bet he thought I would return with Michael, and that everything would go back to normal," Alexa said.

"Your father is a strong man," the queen said. "He will understand. He will not leave you again."

Alexa breathed a heavy sigh.

The queen looked up at her. "Would you like me to explain it to him?"

Alexa shook her head. "No. I'll do it. It'll be easier coming from me."

"Selfless, as always," said the little girl, smiling.

A sudden thought occurred to Alexa. "I just realized something."

"Yes?" said the queen.

"Your name."

The little girl beamed at her. "What is my name?"

"The only power the world has against its evils...is hope. Your name is Hope," she said.

The little girl let out a light, airy laugh. "You are worthy and wise, Alexa Flynn."

EPILOGUE

In a distant land, far to the east of the Eckerly farm, twilight fell on a barren desert. The horizon was edged in red as the light failed. A small bush with dry, brown leaves waved feebly as the final afternoon wind gave one last gust and died out.

A vulture circled low to the ground, swooping on to a small shape that lay still on the horizon. The vulture looked ominous against the darkening sky.

When the breeze died, there was silence for a long while.

Then suddenly, soft footsteps could be heard padding across the rocky wasteland. A hooded figure emerged out of the darkness. He walked slowly and carefully over the broken ground.

The figure stopped and looked to the horizon. He shook his head and the hood fell to his shoulders.

Michael Flynn's face was handsome, but there was a sneering coldness in the eyes that made it less so. His cheeks were hollowed and his face was thin. His lips looked startlingly red against the pallor of his face.

Michael's dark hair was longer than it had ever been — it was sleek and shining against the night sky.

He shook out the sleeve of his robe and in his bony hand he held a book—a green leather-bound tome with stiff pages of yellowing parchment.

Michael brought his other hand over the book and found the spot he was looking for. He struggled to see in the failing light, and kept his finger on the page as he read the instructions once more.

It wasn't far now.

Michael walked for another hour, and finally came to the outcropping of rock that he'd read about so many times. He noticed that the front was jagged and would be difficult to climb, but just beyond that he saw the plateau where he knew the temple stood.

He took a cursory glance down at the book in his hand, but it was too dark to read now.

It didn't matter. Michael knew the words by heart.

"Elbis Fel Wulde," he spoke quietly into the gathering dark.

Michael knew immediately it had worked. He could feel the power of magic surrounding him, and he stared hard at the plateau just beyond the jagged rocks before him.

The image of the empty rock wavered for a moment, and suddenly, a squat, rectangular building appeared before him. The figured sandstone shone against the darkness, and Michael saw the dome settled on top, directly beneath a set of four stars, forming a diamond in the night sky.

Michael began the slow climb over the jagged rocks toward the Temple of Kuln.

As he reached the plateau, he put out his hands and pulled himself forward onto the flat ground. He walked slowly toward the single door, set in the middle of the building. There was an ornate carving of a hand with four fingers on it.

Michael knew from the image in Violet's book that the

fourth finger was severed, but here in the carving it looked as if the image had simply been worn by the sun and dry wind.

He approached the door and closed his eyes in concentration. Then he said, "Dragar."

The door slowly began to open. It scraped loudly on the rock. Michael looked behind him but could see no movement in the shadows.

Once the door was open, he entered quickly. It shut behind him.

Michael found himself in a small, roughly made hallway with a low ceiling. He had to walk through the passage with his head bowed.

There were no torches in the sconces on the walls, but a yellowish glow seemed to emanate from the walls themselves, lighting Michael's way.

He finally came to heavy wooden door at the end of the passage. He knocked.

"Enter," a low voice said.

Michael opened the door and entered a circular room. Michael looked up and realized that the room was exactly beneath the dome he'd observed when the temple first appeared. He looked around. There were no torches here either, but the same yellowish glow showed him his surroundings. There was a large fire pit in the center of the room. The embers were glowing softly. The fire was going out.

Beyond it, Michael could make out five ornately carved stone chairs. The fourth one was cracked and broken down the middle. It was little more than a pile of rocks, and was barely recognizable as a match to the other four seats around it.

Only one seat was occupied. Far to the left, next to the broken chair, a wiry man sat watching Michael Flynn. He had quick intelligent eyes and a strong jaw. There was a look of amused curiosity on his face as he stared at Michael, taking in the young man's height, shining dark hair, and sneering face.

The man in the chair swept fair hair from his eyes and spoke in a ringing voice. "Welcome to the Temple of Kuln. I am Cyril, the fourth brother. Who are you?"

Michael stared at the wiry man and took a long time to answer. Finally, he drew himself up to his fullest height and said, "I am Michael Flynn. I am here to claim my place in the brotherhood."

Cyril laughed softly, but Michael saw his shoulders tense. "You are mistaken, Michael. There is no place for you in the brotherhood. Each of the brothers is alive and well, and in full possession of his power," he said. "You would do well to return upon the death of any of the brothers and make your claim then."

Michael's mind raced automatically to a spell. His fingers itched to release the energy of destruction that pulsed within them. He closed his eyes and took a deep breath, trying to maintain control.

He opened his eyes and looked at Cyril once more.

"I am not a patient man."

About the Author

Patrick Iovinelli teaches courses in language, literature, and science fiction at a large public high school. He is also a musician, baseball fanatic, and little brother. He lives in the Chicago suburbs with his wife, two daughters, and a beagle.

CPSIA information can be obtained
at www.ICGtesting.com
Printed in the USA
LVHW091521210719
624773LV00004B/451/P

9 781949 812053